PEONIES AND POISON

PORT DANBY COZY MYSTERY #7

LONDON LOVETT

WILD FOX PRESS

Peonies and Poison

ISBN-13: 978-1725745674

ISBN-10: 1725745674

CHAPTER 1

So much blinding white heat reflected off the sidewalk, I half expected my sandal to get mired in sticky cement. A heat wave had roared into town two days earlier and it seemed even the cooling ocean breeze had given up trying to compete with the determined sun.

I took another sip of the strawberry, banana and yogurt smoothie I'd blended for breakfast and plodded toward the shop. Cooking anything on the stove or in the oven had been out of the question in my tiny house. I'd resorted to salads, sandwiches and all things that were refreshing and blend-worthy.

Kingston flew ahead but arced quickly to the ground when he spotted Elsie standing out at her sidewalk tables. My bird knew the small, fast moving woman with the gray and toffee hair was always a sure bet for a cookie or muffin crumb. To Kinston's disappointment, the box Elsie carried contained batteries and mini handheld fans.

Elsie glanced toward Kingston as he paced anxiously on the hot cement, still holding out hope that there were scones buried beneath the batteries. She placed the box on one of her tables and scanned the sidewalk.

Her white smile flashed my direction. "I saw the crow and figured the owner wasn't far behind."

I pressed the smoothie cup against my cheek. "I can't believe it's this hot already."

"Never felt anything like it. It's actually cooler in my kitchen, with four convection ovens blasting baked goods, then it is out here on the sidewalk. Smart that you left your bike at home today." Elsie pulled a tiny fan from the box and started putting batteries into its base.

"I tried to convince myself I was tough enough to handle the bike ride to town but the second I stepped outside, I raced back in for my keys."

Elsie shrugged. "You've got to get out before the sun comes up. I ran five miles before I opened up at dawn and the temperature was lovely."

"Yes, well, you are super woman and I'm the mild mannered florist who doesn't rise from bed until I can see sunlight peeping around the drapes."

Kingston waddled under the table we were standing at but even the shade of the table top wasn't enough to cool the cement. He danced back and forth impatiently, waiting to get inside to his perch.

"That poor bird is stuck wearing head to toe black." Elsie turned the fan on. I closed my eyes as a small blast of air hit my face." What do you think?"

"I guess the Great Table War is back on. I thought you two had grown bored of competing." Elsie and Les had taken sibling rivalry to a whole new level with their sidewalk sitting areas, but I doubted the fancy furniture and even the small handheld fans would convince people to sit out on the blistering sidewalk. Even the trees lining Harbor Lane looked as if they wanted to be anywhere but standing on the city street.

"I've told you before, it's not a competition." Elsie scoffed. "Clearly, people prefer to sit in front of the bakery. Who can resist sitting in the swirl of cinnamon, sugar and spice drifting out from my shop?"

I tapped my chin. "Hmm, maybe people who prefer to sit in the swirl of rich roasted coffee aroma. I don't think anything will entice people to sit on either side this week. At least not until the sweltering temperatures are gone."

Ignoring my prediction, Elsie went right on dropping batteries into the fans.

Footsteps grabbed both our attentions. Ryder strolled past staring at his phone and looking more than a little distracted. His sunglasses were shoved on his head and his mouth was set in a firm line. He didn't notice us, or the crow who immediately trotted his direction.

"Kids and their phones." Elsie clucked her tongue. "The entire world could be burning down around them and they wouldn't notice because they'd be too focused on their friend's latest Instagram picture of the world going up in flames."

I watched as my normally astute and dialed in assistant continued on without even a glance our direction. "That's strange. I know a lot of people are glued to their phones but it's not like Ryder. Something must be up." I turned to Elsie. "Anyhow, I need to get inside. I've got a future bride coming in this morning to pick flowers for the bridal bouquets. I'll see you later. And good luck with the fans."

"Thanks."

Kingston startled Ryder as he unlocked the flower shop. The crow flew past him and headed straight for his perch beneath the air conditioning vent.

"You'll have to excuse his rude behavior," I said from behind, startling Ryder again.

"Hey, boss," he said with mild enthusiasm. Something was definitely up and I was certain it had to do with my capricious best friend. Lola seemed pleased about their relationship. At the same time, she occasionally had that nervous deer look on her face as if she was just waiting for one sign of danger so she could run for the hills.

I followed him inside and walked straight to the thermostat on the back wall. "It's already eighty degrees in here." I flicked the switch on. The drumming sound of the air conditioner rumbled through ducts over head. "I have a feeling the electric bill is going to surpass my profits this week, but I have to keep the shop cool for the flowers and customers."

"Or you could turn it into a big greenhouse." Even his usual smile was weak. "Has the bride picked the kind of flower she wants?"

"Yes, she wants peonies. I created a few examples last night before I closed up. Hopefully, one of them will work."

Ryder followed me down the short hallway to the office. His footsteps didn't have the usual bounce.

I put my purse away and turned on my computer. Ryder glanced at his phone once more before pushing it into his pocket.

"Anything wrong?" I asked hesitantly. I knew having my best friend and my coworker in a relationship was going to add a layer of trouble to my close knit social circle but I had only myself to blame. I'd pushed and prodded and hinted about them getting together so much, I could easily have earned the title of meddling matchmaker.

"Everything is just peachy," Ryder said dryly.

"Since you're throwing around words like peachy, I'm going to assume things are anything but peachy." I walked out behind him.

"Lola is going to France," he blurted the words quickly, as if they left a bitter taste in his mouth.

Lola's parents had rented a cottage in France. They told her they would pay for her plane ticket if she wanted to join them. The last time she'd mentioned it to me, she seemed dead set against it. She must have changed her mind.

"I'm sure she won't be gone long." It was a lame response to make him feel better, but it was the only thing that popped into my head.

Ryder swung around. "So you knew about her trip?"

"Huh? No, not really. She mentioned that her parents offered to fly her to France but last we spoke, she'd decided not to go." My words rushed out as if I was making them up as I went but they were true. I smiled weakly at him. "She won't stay long, Ryder. Besides, you know the old saying—"

"If you're going to say absence makes the heart grow fonder, I should warn you that my mom already threw that pearl of wisdom my way and it bounced right off my hard head. Lola will forget all about me when she's dashing around the dazzling French coastline and traveling the countryside. And I wouldn't blame her either. What am I compared to the sights, smells and sounds of France?"

I put my hand on his arm. "As far as I'm concerned the sights, smells and sounds of Ryder Kirkland are just as exciting." His bunched brows mirrored mine. "Yes, now that I've heard that aloud, it didn't quite work the way I expected."

A smile finally broke on his face. It seemed I'd temporarily humored him out of his moment of self-doubt. "I'll get started on the bouquets for the Woman's Club luncheon," Ryder said. "And I promise not to sulk. Not too much, anyhow."

"That's the spirit." I headed to the refrigerator and pulled out the four bridal bouquet samples I'd created. One was a simple bouquet of pale pink peony buds mixed in with full white blooms. I left the stems long and bare and wrapped them with burlap. A second bouquet was a more formal mix of pink peonies and yellow roses. White baby's breath sprigs lent a whimsical touch. I'd pulled together a striking monochromatic bouquet of double pink peonies and tied them off with a white satin ribbon. It was vibrant with color and fragrance. The last bouquet was a country charm mix of pale pink peonies and yellow buttercups framed by lacy green fern. With any luck, the bride would know exactly which one would fit seamlessly into the occasion.

CHAPTER 2

A baby blue Fiat parked in front of the shop. I'd only spoken to Jazmin, the bride-to-be, on the phone once, but she struck me as decisive and confident. She knew she wanted peonies in her bouquets because they were her grandmother's favorite.

The door swung open and two young women were chatting away as they walked inside. It was easy to spot the future bride. She had that radiant glow of a woman immersed in a fantasy world of satin and lace and everything bridal. Or it might have been the brutal hot streaks of sunlight pouring down from the sky. She was clutching a bottle of vitamin water in one hand and an oversized designer handbag in the other. A tiny head of gray curls popped up from inside the bag. The teacup poodle had a quick look around the store, sneezed twice and then dropped back into its hiding place. The second woman, who appeared much closer to her teens than to adulthood, skittered across the floor in her sandals and white cut off shorts.

"Look, Jazzy! I heard they had a crow inside this shop." The girl had hair the color of caramel. Long fringy bangs hung close to her blue eyes. She looked across the store at me. "Is he friendly?" she asked.

I'd found it best practice to not let strangers touch Kingston. As domesticated as he was, I never knew exactly how he was going to react to someone new. And most people tended to just shoot their hand straight at him, not considering that it might startle him.

"Kingston loves people," I said. "But he prefers to be admired from a distance."

"Come on, Trinity. We don't have time to dawdle. I'm meeting Bradley for lunch in Mayfield." The bride walked directly to the peony bouquets on the work island and placed her handbag on the floor next to her feet.

"Hello." I reached my hand out. "I'm Lacey, the shop owner. You must be Jazmin."

She took my hand. Her nails had tiny flowers painted across the tips. "Yes, I'm the one you spoke to on the phone." The younger girl had lost her interest in Kingston and joined us at the island. She hopped up on a stool. "This is my sister, Trinity. She's supposed to be helping me, but, well . . ." Jazmin scowled at her sister, who responded with an eye roll.

"Whatever, Jazzy. It's just that you can't make up your mind about anything. We spent like three years in the print shop picking out her invitations. Then she changed her mind ten minutes after we left the store."

Jazmin had dark, expressive brows. They were showing frustration. "Sure, three years. It was two hours at the most."

"Nope, nope, nope." Trinity shook her head. She shot me a serious glance. "I walked into the shop with short bangs and left with these." She pointed to her overlong bangs and then swept them away from her forehead. Her blue eyes landed on the peonies. "These are so pretty. Grammie is going to love them."

Jazmin seemed less enamored with the bouquets. She pursed her lips and tilted her head from side to side. She backed up and squinted at the bouquets.

Trinity blew a puff of air straight up, ruffling her long bangs. "Why are you backing away from the flowers and doing this?" Trinity squished up her nose and squinted her eyes. She laughed and fished for her phone. "I should get a picture of you with that goofy face."

Jazmin shook her head and sighed audibly. "Do you see what I mean?" she asked me.

I didn't respond. I already spent my entire workday between the king and queen of sibling rivalry. I certainly didn't need to step between two sisters.

"If you must know, Trini, I'm trying to see how the flowers will look from a distance. It's a big church. I want the people in the back to see them. I should take a few pictures to send to Mom." Jazmin's tiny dog squeaked and stuck his nose out of the purse while she searched for her phone. She set to work taking pictures of the bouquets from every angle as if she were doing a photo shoot for a florist instead of picking her wedding bouquets.

I patted the counter. "I'll let you decide then. Just let me know if there's a combination you like or would prefer to see."

Ryder came out from the store room with a large bag of potting soil draped over his shoulder. Trinity sat up perkily on the stool. "Hello," she chirped across the store.

"Good morning," he said politely back.

Trinity leaned forward and dropped her voice to a whisper. "He's cute. Does he work here?"

Before I could answer, Jazmin piped up with a short laugh. "No, she just pulled him in off the street to carry dirt around the store." As hard as Jazmin was trying to be the mature, soon to be married, older sister it seemed she couldn't resist a sarcastic sisterly barb.

9

"Ryder does work here," I added. "He's a great assistant."

Trinity repositioned herself on the stool. "He's cute but too old. I only just turned eighteen. Besides, I have a boyfriend." She quickly swiped through the photos on her phone and showed me a picture. A pillbox style red usher's hat squashed down the teen's curly sun bleached hair. He had his thumb and pinky raised in the hang loose gesture. "His name is Justin. He doesn't usually wear that stupid looking theater usher uniform. I mean he dresses cool, like a surfer, when he's not stuck in the uniform." She lowered the phone. "We both work at the Mayfield Four Movie Theater. Have you been there?"

I couldn't remember the last time I'd been to the movies. Briggs had suggested it a few times but then we always had a hard time agreeing on a movie. "I haven't seen a movie in a long time," I said. "But in this heat wave, I'll bet it's a great place to hang out for a few hours."

"For sure." Trinity kicked her suntanned legs back and forth. "Especially because we have the best slush making machine for miles. We just added a new flavor too. Lemon-lime. It's super tasty."

"Hmm, lemon-lime sounds good." I flicked my attention her sister's direction. She was still taking pictures. "I'll have to check out the movie listings to see if there's anything my boyfriend—" I paused. I suddenly realized I had yet to call Briggs my boyfriend. It sounded strange to my ear.

Trinity's laugh pulled me from my thoughts. "I know what you mean. Justin and I can't ever decide on a movie. I like horror movies and he likes superhero flicks."

"But I'll bet you get to see them all for free so you can see anything you want."

She shook her head and her long bangs fell over her eyes. She brushed them aside. "I wish. Our boss, Mr. Samuels, is *soo* stingy. He only gives us a ten percent discount on the snack bar. Even then, he watches us like crazy to make sure we're not eating or drinking too much. The only time we see the movies for free is when we have to walk in and tell some bratty kids to be quiet or ask someone to stop throwing popcorn at the screen."

"That's too bad. It seems like a free movie, or at the very least, a free box of licorice should be one of the perks of the job."

"All right." Jazmin finally put down her phone. "I really like this one." She pointed out the bouquet with pink peonies and yellow buttercups.

"Great. The buttercups are hard to come by at this time of year, but I'm sure I can track some down. They might be a little more money though."

Jazmin waved off the mention of money. "Daddy said I could pick whatever I like."

Trinity clucked her tongue and hopped off the stool. "Oh brother. I ask for a new phone and he throws a fit." She wandered across the room to the work area where Ryder was cutting flowers for bouquets. He didn't seem to mind the company. Apparently there was nothing like a cute girl to take your mind off relationship problems.

Jazmin picked up the bouquet and moved it around, circling it through the air. She was a very thorough flower shopper. The dance act caught her sister's attention. Trinity's giggles filled the shop. "Are you going to be walking down the aisle like that?" She stuck one hand on her hip and performed an exaggerated bridal walk across the shop waving her invisible bouquet around as she went.

Jazmin ignored her sister's antics. "I wonder if it's a little heavy."

"I could lighten it up by putting in more greenery and leaving out some of the peonies."

Her mouth swished back and forth in thought. "No, I think maybe less of the yellow flowers. I want the peonies to stay the star of the show." She laughed lightly and pointed to herself. "Other than the bride, of course."

"Naturally. And you'll make a very beautiful bride at that."

My comment earned a scoffing sound from Trinity, who had joined us at the counter.

I circled around to the back side of the work island and pulled out my order book. "Great. I'll keep the peonies for your bouquet at ten and reduce the yellow buttercups to four. How many bridesmaids will there be?"

"She doesn't know because her two best friends have been fighting over the maid of honor spot." Trinity said with a spoonful of derision added on top. "Doesn't it seem right that her only sister should be the maid of honor?" she asked me.

Jazmin elbowed her aside. "No, it isn't right. But it's true. I have two best friends and I'm having a hard time deciding. But there will be six altogether, including the little sister that my parents insisted had to be part of the bridal party—"Jazmin curled a scowl Trinity's way.

Trinity picked up one of the bouquets and ran her fingers over the soft petals. "She's just worried I'll outshine her on her wedding day."

Jazmin plucked the bouquet from Trinity and placed it on the counter. "Why don't you go talk to the bird while we finish the order."

Trinity's phone buzzed. "That's probably Justin. He's looking for another job because of horrible Mr. Samuels," she said to no one in particular.

Jazmin sighed in relief as her sister walked away with the phone. "Teenagers are always such big shots. I don't think I ever acted like her."

I smiled and glanced across the store at Trinity. She was rocking back and forth on her heels while she texted on her phone. "I think I acted a lot like your sister. She's fun but then I'm not her big sister. I'm sure my opinion would be different in that circumstance." I continued with the order. The wedding was in early fall so I'd have to contact my supplier right away to get in my order. Neither flower was easy to come by at that time of year but I'd partnered up with a number of hothouse suppliers who could get me virtually any bloom I wanted. Even in fall and winter.

Trinity's sandals slapped the floor dejectedly. "Poor Justin didn't get the job at the warehouse. They wanted someone with experience."

"Too bad surfing doesn't come in handy for job skills," Jazmin sniped before walking away to answer her phone.

"Just because Bradley is a computer nerd doesn't mean I can't date someone cool," Trinity said to her sister's back. She climbed back on the stool, stuck her elbows on the island and her chin on her hands. "I guess he's stuck working at the theater. Mr. Samuels really hates Justin. He yells at him about everything." Trinity went on with her one-sided conversation. I politely nodded but I was concentrating on writing the order. She slapped the counter suddenly, startling me into a mistake. I crossed out the nine that should have been a six.

"Sorry about that," Trinity said. "But I just thought I'd let you know about vintage movie night. It's tomorrow night at seven. We're screening Casablanca. I've never seen it but I've heard it's one of those cool old black and white flicks."

"Here's looking at you kid," I muttered absently.

Trinity blinked at me. "Huh?"

"Oh, that's from the movie. It's a classic. And that line is probably the most famous movie quote of all time." I stopped and tapped my pen on the order pad. "Did you say it starts at seven?"

She straightened her posture, excited that she'd caught my interest. "Sally Applegate, the assistant manager sets up cool events like vintage movie night. She does an awesome job. You'd think Mr. Samuels would pat her on the back and tell her good job, or at least give her a free soda for her effort, but nope. He's as stingy and mean as they come."

"He does sound like a terrible man to work for."

"Do you think you might come? Ask your boyfriend. It's nice and cool inside the theater and don't forget to try the lemon-lime slush."

"Actually, that does sound fun. Thanks for letting me know."

CHAPTER 3

$\mathcal{T}$he sweltering temperatures of the morning had amped up to the blistering, searing heat of mid afternoon. The air was thick and gooey as I headed along Harbor Lane to the Port Danby Police Station. It felt like I was wading through a viscous vat of syrup. The high temperature had burned off any coastal breeze. The usual odors wafting up from the marina, including the fishing boats, were extra pungent. Kingston hadn't left his perch inside the air conditioned shop all day and I could hardly blame him. If I hadn't been invited to lunch by my favorite local detective, I might have stayed huddled inside too.

The door to the police station opened a good twenty feet before I reached it. Briggs' dog, Bear, came galumphing out. It seemed every time the pup's body finally grew into his long legs and massive ears, his limbs and ears grew again, leaving him more room to catch up. He was in the silly, gangly teenager stage.

I stooped down and let him lick my chin as I rubbed his soft fur. His owner's shadow loomed over us, providing us with a much needed touch of shade for our greeting.

I stood up straight. "Don't take this the wrong way, but I think your dog might be part cartoon. Sometimes he looks more like an animated character in a kid's movie than an actual dog."

Briggs laughed. He always looked extra sharp with his shirt sleeves rolled up. He was still dressed for work but a tie and coat were out of the question today. "I have to agree. I had to bring him to work today because the air conditioner overheated in my house last night and it's like an oven."

"That's terrible. What a time for the thing to overheat. Although, I guess that wouldn't happen unless it was running nonstop."

"Since I've got my animated nuisance along for lunch, I thought we'd just pick up a hot dog on the pier. Maybe walk down to the water. It has to be at least a few degrees cooler near the ocean."

"Sounds good to me. I'm starved. My house has no air conditioner to overheat, so I've been relying solely on the rare breeze to blow through. I haven't turned on the oven or stove for a few days and I've been mostly drinking my meals. Sinking my teeth into solid food is just what I need."

"Jeez, and here I am complaining about my broken air conditioner."

"Yes but I can feel the ocean breeze at my house." I was tempted to take his arm but it was too hot even for that. "Although, it seems the afternoon breeze has hightailed it for cooler shores. Which reminds me, I've got an idea for a movie date."

We reached the pier. Bear galloped enthusiastically up the steps ahead of us.

"Bear, sit," Briggs called. The dog reached the landing and sat down obediently. But his tail swished excitedly from side to side at the prospect of terrifying pigeons and gulls.

"Impressive," I noted. "He's come a long way." I glanced over at Briggs. The faint lines on the side of his mouth seemed to indicate he was holding back a proud grin.

"I have to admit, it's nice having a dog again."

This time, hot or not, I reached over and curled my arm around his. "It suits you. You look even better with a big furry pal strutting next to you."

His brown eyes flicked sideways at me. "Even better? I like that. I'll have to bring him to work more often." Right as he said it, Bear loped ahead scattering a group of industrious pigeons into the air, which, in turn, caused a woman to startle and drop her ice cream cone, scoop first, onto the pier.

Briggs reached for his wallet. "Or maybe not." He hurried ahead and quickly apologized for the dog as he handed her money for another cone. Bear *sacrificed* his pigeon chase to clean up the ice cream mess.

The heat wave had given everyone the same idea as us. The pier was crowded with people looking for a cooler spot to have lunch. But without the breeze, there wouldn't be much of a reprieve.

I crinkled my nose in an attempt to tamp down my extra acute sense of smell. Most of the time, the coastline was ripe with the fresh, salty scent of the ocean. Today, the mix of aromas and odors was overwhelming. As hungry as I was, even a hot dog didn't sound appetizing.

Bear finished lapping up the ice cream and was busy flicking his tongue across his wet, black nose to get the last drops as Briggs finished his apology.

"Bear, here." He pointed to his side. For the first time since the ice cream calamity, the dog seemed to gather that he was in trouble. He dropped his head and tail and wiggled his hips as he shuffled over to us. "I should have brought his leash."

"He's fine," I assured Briggs. "Besides, I think you made that woman's day with your chivalrous apology. I'm sure she wasn't expecting it. However, the ice cream fiasco has sort of made me change my mind about the hot dog. I think I'll lick my lunch."

"You're going to eat ice cream for lunch?" he asked.

I twitched my nose. "Samantha can't seem to switch off all the pungent odors on the pier today. The hot air has magnified everything. It has sort of ruined my appetite." Briggs had come up with the nickname Samantha for my nose since I moved it like the character in the vintage television show Bewitched.

"I'm sorry, Lacey. I shouldn't have suggested the beach for lunch." He wore concern so genuinely (and handsomely) on his face it made me smile.

"Nonsense. I'll enjoy lunch no matter where we are as long as I'm with two of my favorite guys." I patted Bear's head to let him know he was included in the list. "I think super nose or not, I'd still be craving ice cream. It's just too hot for anything else. Go buy your hot dog and get me a scoop of that lemon gelato. In fact, make it a double. Bear and I will wait for you."

"Right. Double scoop of lemon gelato." He instructed Bear to stay. The dog sat down next to me but his tail wagged with frustration. He badly wanted to follow Briggs. It was a true friendship. Or it might have been because Briggs was heading to the hot dog stand.

A few minutes later, Briggs had his hot dog and I had my bowl of gelato. The creamy treat was tart and lush and refreshing in my mouth. And the strong citrus scent was doing an admirable job competing with the strong odors circulating around my nose.

We headed down the end of the pier and toward the sandy path to Pickford Beach. School was several weeks away and the sand was dotted with kids playing volleyball and hanging out with friends. The water was more crowded than I'd seen it all summer with people splashing, swimming and keeping cool in the waves.

"So you mentioned a movie date?" Briggs led me to a bench near the path and we sat down to eat. Bear crawled beneath the shade of the bench but I was certain he was keeping a close eye on the group of seagulls strutting around the sand in front of us.

I swallowed another bite of the silky gelato. "Yes. I had a bridal order this morning and the bride's sister mentioned that she worked at Mayfield Four Movie Theater. Hates her boss, by the way, but that's another story. Anyhow, they are having a special screening of Casablanca tomorrow night. Are you interested?"

"Are you asking me out on a date, Miss Pinkerton?" he teased.

"As a matter of fact, yes, I am, Detective Briggs. My treat. I'll even spring for the lemon-lime slush drinks, which I've been assured are delicious. I'm mostly drawn to the idea that theaters are always just a touch too cold. In any case, it'll be much cooler than my house."

"A little Bogie in the air conditioning. Sounds good." Briggs wiped some mustard off the corner of his mouth. Now that we were clear of the unpleasant aromas on the pier, the hot dog looked pretty tasty. Apparently he caught me gazing longingly at his relish and mustard topped bun. He lifted it for me to take a bite. Which I did.

"Hmm, yep, should have gotten a hot dog."

Briggs scooted forward. "I'll go up and get you one."

"No, don't worry about it. So it's a date. The movie starts at seven tomorrow."

"Great. I'll pick you up at half past six. Should I wear a fedora and trench coat?"

"Only if you want me to keep favoring you with my Ingrid Bergman smoldering, starry-eyed gaze."

"I could put up with a little smolder and stars." Briggs handed Bear the last bite of hot dog and took a drink of soda. "Interestingly enough, last fall I had to deal with a theater feud between the owner of Mayfield Four and the owner of Starlight Movie Theater across town. Apparently, there's always been a good dose of rivalry between the theaters. Then one night, after closing thankfully, the Starlight Theater had a fire. The source was determined to be a faulty plug on the pretzel warmer. No one was hurt but the damage was significant. The owner, Connie Wilkerson, had to close up the theater for months. She nearly lost everything in the process, but she's back up and running. From what I've heard, it's been nearly impossible for her to compete now. Which brings me to the trouble. Miss Wilkerson came to me alleging that Ronald Samuels, the owner of Mayfield Four, had started the fire or at least hired someone to start it. There wasn't any evidence to support her claim so she had to drop the matter. She wasn't happy."

"I'll bet. I know Trinity, the girl who told me about the Casablanca screening, had nothing but terrible things to say about Mr. Samuels. He sounds like a hard man to work for."

Briggs carried our trash to the nearest can, and we started our walk back to work. It seemed the whole world was moving in slow motion due to the heat. Three boys on bicycles pedaled along the planks of the pier as if they were dragging wagons of bricks behind their bikes. People strolled slowly and closely to the railing trying hard to catch a cooling mist from the water below. Most of the pigeons and gulls that milled about the food stands had taken off to shady trees or the cool grass beneath the lighthouse. Even Bear's earlier exuberant prance had been replaced with a sluggish, plodding trot.

"My phone says the heat wave might break this weekend," I said. "I'll be ready for it."

"Me too. One good thing, the excessive heat always seems to tamp down crime. Guess people are too hot to get into trouble."

"Really? Interesting. Well, if we're going to be murder and crime free in our fair town for awhile, then I should get back to the Hawksworth case. I want to keep my detective skills sharp and ready for the next moment of mayhem."

"Have you learned anything new?" Briggs took my hand. I loved the protective way he squeezed my fingers. My heart skipped a beat or two. I let it get back to normal before focusing on his question.

"Did I tell you about the letters I found in the trunk inside the gardener's shed?"

"You mean the Hawksworth Museum you break into every chance you get?"

Bear insisted on pushing between us, making it impossible to continue holding hands. We parted as we turned the corner onto Harbor Lane.

"Yes, but I don't think you can call it a break in when the lock just slides open. Anyhow, are you interested in my very interesting find, or not?"

Briggs smiled my direction. I wondered if he knew the power behind that grin. "Yes, I'm interested. Continue."

"First of all, the trunk is not a hope chest. It's filled with a man's ascots and straw boaters. I'm sure the items belonged to Bertram Hawksworth. In fact, his business ledgers are stored inside."

"Really? Anything of note inside the ledgers?" Bear trotted ahead and sat in front of the police station door, apparently anxious to get back into the air conditioning.

"Lots of numbers in columns. Just what you'd expect. But I did discover something. I'm just not sure if it's anything important." We stopped in front of the station. Briggs opened the door and Bear darted inside.

"Pampered pooch," I mused.

"Said the woman whose pet crow has his own collection of treats, custom perches and gets to decide the day's agenda."

"Touché. Back to the ledgers. I'll talk fast because I need to get back to the shop. According to the signatures in the account ledgers, it seemed Jane Price, Mayor Harvard Price's daughter from his first marriage, worked as Bertram Hawkworth's accountant for a short time."

Briggs stared at me expectantly, apparently waiting for a bigger shoe to drop.

"That's the interesting part," I said, hesitantly. "Mayor Harvard Price, great-grandfather of the current Mayor price," I added.

"Yes, I made the connection. We detectives are good at things like that. But what does it have to do with the murder?"

I raised a dramatic brow. "Yes. What indeed?"

"So you found a connection?"

"Well, no. Not exactly."

Hilda poked her head outside. "Dear me, it's like sticking my head in the oven to check if the roast is done," she quipped.

"Oh, it's done," I said. "In fact, I'd say it's well done. How are you, Hilda?"

"Aside from being sticky from head to toe, I'm fine. Thank you."

I nodded. "This weather makes everything sticky."

Hilda's round cheeks turned to apples. "No, I'm sticky because that big, slobbery dog just licked me from head to toe as if we'd been parted for weeks." She looked over at Briggs. "I've finished typing those reports. I was going to take off early. My sister is having a pool party."

"Absolutely, Hilda. Enjoy yourself. Uh, Hilda," Briggs said quickly before she closed the door.

She popped her head back out. This time Bear's head came with it. "Yes?"

"Is Officer Chinmoor on the schedule tomorrow night?"

"I'll double check but I think so."

"Great. Thanks."

Hilda and Bear withdrew their faces from the hot outside air. Briggs turned to me. He had that sparkle in his brown eyes that tended to make my knees turn to gelatin. "Then I guess the date is on for sure." He clipped me lightly on the chin. "Here's lookin' at you, kid." It was an impressive impersonation of Bogart and it added to the wobble in my knees.

"We'll always have Paris," I replied. "But I guess we'd have to go to Paris first for that line to have meaning."

"Maybe someday. Have a nice afternoon, Miss Pinkerton."

"You too, Detective Briggs."

CHAPTER 4

*R*yder had moped around most of the afternoon. He left early for a swim at the beach and I finished with my paperwork. The shop had been close to deserted most of the day. My offer of free air conditioning and flowery fragrances wasn't enough to entice people out for a day of flower shopping. It was just too hot to think about anything except staying cool.

Kingston had finished his lunch and was sleeping soundly on his perch. Something told me he was dreaming of swooping through red and gold trees on a blustery fall day. He was not a summer lover. Like Elsie had noted—the poor guy was clad head to toe in black.

I left him to his bird dreams and locked up for a few minutes to walk across the street. Lola's shop looked as deserted as mine, so it seemed we'd have an opportunity to chat. I had more than a few questions to ask.

Lola was stooped down below the counter. Her red hair peeked up over the display of vintage lighters. "When were you going to let your best friend know that you were flying halfway across the world to France?" I asked as I headed toward the counter.

The thick red hair emerged and a face came with it, only it wasn't the one I was expecting. The red haired girl behind the counter looked to be in her early twenties. Her skin was paler than Lola's and her eyes were blue instead of brown. But there was something about her expression that reminded me of Lola. She found her tongue before me.

"Oh, you're the pretty lady who runs the flower shop. I saw you this morning with your crow. Lo-lo told me all about your pet crow, Kingston. I can't wait to meet him." Before I could say hello, she scrambled on about my bird. "Although, if I'm being honest, they kind of scare me with those long sharp beaks and beady black eyes. Is he really as friendly as Lo-lo says?" Sleuth that I was, I quickly determined the loving nickname Lo-lo, the red hair and the similar expressions meant I was talking to Lola's relative.

"I'm Lacey, owner of Pink's Flowers. You must be—" I paused for her to fill in the name. It took her a second to understand.

"Oh right, I'm Shauna. I'm Lo-lo's cousin. Our moms are sisters."

"Wonderful. I didn't know you were visiting. Nice to meet you. And Kingston can be shy around strangers but he is extra friendly to your cousin." I leaned in for a conspiratorial whisper, figuring Lola was just a few feet away in her office. "My crow has a huge crush on Lola."

"That's right. I attract all kinds," Lola said as she stepped into the shop front. She was carrying a box with glass trinkets.

I put my hands on my hips. "How on earth did you hear that? Sometimes I think we should combine my sense of smell with your sense of hearing and start some kind of—" They both waited for me to finish, but I couldn't come up with anything clever.

"Superhero club?" Lola provided with a wry smile as she placed the box on the counter.

"Yes, a club for super senses." I turned to her cousin. "Are you in town long?"

Shauna parted her lips to answer but Lola stepped in first. "She's here to run the store and house sit while I'm in France."

I leaned my arm on the counter and turned to face her. "Yes, I've heard rumors of you jetting off to Europe. Normally, it's something one would expect to hear straight from one's best friend but—"

"Why are you talking in the third person?" I could tell instantly that Lola wasn't excited or anxious for the trip. Her mouth was turned down at the edges and her shoulders were rounded. "And I won't be gone long. My parents, me and a small cottage does not spell success or a long vacation. I give it three days and I'll be packing up for the airport." Lola started removing the glassware from the box. Most of it was green and muted orange depression glass. The low cost plates and cups that were manufactured and distributed during the Great Depression. "Are you going to miss me?" she asked with a laugh.

"Hmm, that depends. Are you going to bring your best friend back something pretty from France?"

"I could probably find some pretty trinket that my best friend will like."

Lola handed Shauna a green cake plate and pointed to the dust cloth near the cash register. Shauna picked it up and absently wiped the glass as she listened to our amusing chatter.

"In that case, yes, I'll miss you a great deal. But maybe not as much as a certain someone who has been doing more than his share of brooding today."

Lola glanced swiftly toward her cousin and motioned for me to follow her to the office.

Shauna's posture slumped when she realized she wasn't going to get to hear the rest of the conversation.

Lola waved me past her into her tiny office nook. "I don't need

Shauna listening in," she said quietly and shut the door. "She relays everything to her mom, my Aunt Ruby, and then Aunt Ruby relays everything to my mom. Only Ruby usually puts her own spin on it. Then the whole thing gets twisted into some sordid tale about me dating the president of a motorcycle club or whatever other fun details get tossed in on the rumor chain."

She leaned against her desk and crossed her arms over the screaming eagle on her Van Halen t-shirt. "Is he really upset?"

"Well, it *was* kind of sudden. Just the other day you mentioned something about rather having a root canal than spending so much time with your parents."

Lola smiled about her analogy. "I guess I did say that. But, you know, my best friend"—She waved her hand toward me—"the oddball who likes to refer to herself in third person, has been such a role model for me. She spent an entire week with her parents and she survived without one meltdown. I thought I'd give it a shot with my own ma and pa." She stared down at the ground then, even though there was nothing of interest on the carpeted floor of her office. Her mouth pursed like a fish and then her chin jutted side to side. All gestures that assured me she had more to say on the subject.

"But . . ." I said as a starting point.

Her thin shoulders poked at the worn cotton t-shirt as she took a deep breath and rested her hands back against the desk. "Not but. *Besides* is a better way to begin. Besides, I think Ryder and I are moving too fast. When I go fast, I tend to lose control. I crash and burn."

"We are talking about relationships and not your terrible driving skills, right?"

"Yes, and I'm not that bad behind the wheel. Ah, who am I kidding? I'm terrible. Yes, I'm talking about my relationship." She put up her hand. "And before you start, Miss Meddlesome Matchmaker, I'm not running away. I'm just putting some space between us. A lot of space actually. And an ocean. So no unwanted advice or prodding."

I shook my head once and pretended to zip my lips, then immediately opened them. "You're right. I was being a meddlesome matchmaker. It's only because I thought you two were absolutely perfect—"

Lola raised her brow at me.

"Oops." I pressed my fingers to my lips but then dropped them quickly. "I guess it's not that easy to drop the matchmaker persona. But I will be the complete opposite of a matchmaker. I'll be a—" I tilted my head to the side. "Does matchmaker have an antonym?"

"Divorce lawyer?" Lola asked and we both burst into laughter.

I stepped forward to hug her. "I really am going to miss you. But I think it's good you're taking a little time for yourself. Well, other than being stuck in a cottage with your parents."

"I plan to do a lot of exploring. I am looking forward to it. I just hope Shauna can handle running the shop. She said some of the old stuff creeps her out. She's always been afraid of everything. Can't tell you how many times we had to cut the trick or treating short because Shauna would see something scary and want to turn back." Lola held up her hands. "I mean, duh. It was Halloween. Scary was kind of the theme. I was thrilled when I was old enough to just go with my friends and leave Shauna behind."

A loud gasp was followed by the sound of glass shattering. Lola's shoulders rose up to her ears. "My mom insisted I let her watch the house and shop. I think it was as a favor to Aunt Ruby, who needed a break from my cousin. But I'm not sure if anything of value will be left by the time I return. That's the third piece she's broken today." Lola headed to the door. "I've got to help her clean up. I don't want Bloomer to get a glass shard in his paw." She stopped before opening the door and lowered her voice to a whisper. "I swear I've caught that dog rolling his eyes twice today. Wait until he learns she's babysitting him for the next week." She opened the door and I followed her out.

Late Bloomer was sitting in front of the counter, watching raptly as Shauna frantically swept up chunks of glass. There was no eye roll but I was sure I caught an amused grin in the folds of his jowl.

Shauna glanced up with round blue eyes. She looked pale with panic about the mishap. "I'm sorry, Lola. The thing just slipped out of my fingers." Her voice wavered as if she might cry.

"Don't worry about it," Lola muttered. She stooped down to pick up the bigger shards.

"I'm so clumsy," Shauna said as she moved the broom back and forth. "Mom calls me butter fingers and she's right. It's like I dip my hands in butter every morning. Only not regular butter. That weird oily stuff they put on movie popcorn."

Lola straightened with a handful of large chunks. "Just make sure your movie popcorn hands get every piece. I don't want Bloomer to step on anything."

"That reminds me," I said as I patted Bloomer on the head. "Briggs and I are going to the Mayfield Four Theater tomorrow night. They're showing Casablanca."

"Sounds serious," Lola quipped. "First Casablanca, then North by Northwest. And before you know it, the two of you are sharing a soda in a Gone with the Wind marathon."

I ruffled Bloomer's soft ears. "Your mom is such a funny woman."

Lola snapped her fingers. "Funny woman. Streisand. No wait. That was Funny Girl."

"I love vintage classic movie night at the Mayfield Four," Shauna chirped. "For Halloween, they always decorate the theater and play one of the creepy black and white monster movies. They're my kind of horror movie because they don't include some awful guy sneaking around with a chainsaw and hockey mask.

Those are way too scary." The broom nearly slipped from her hand as she tried to get some pieces out from under the counter. "Sally Applegate, the assistant manager of the theater—" She paused to bend over and pick up a large chunk. "She sets up the special movie nights. She belongs to the same anxiety support group as me."

Lola turned to her. "I didn't know you were in group therapy."

Shauna shrugged. It seemed she didn't mind talking about it. "Yeah, I was getting these panic attacks whenever something worried me, so Mom thought I should go. The therapist, Miss Nader, is a friend of hers. It really helps. I hardly ever have panic attacks anymore."

"Good to know since I'm putting you in charge of everything," Lola muttered with a good dose of sarcasm. She shot me a secret eye roll. I could easily predict what the first topic of conversation would be between Lola and her mom once she landed in France.

I tapped the counter with my fingers. "Well, I've left Kingston in nap mode. I should get back. He's all alone in the shop."

That statement caught Lola's attention. "Kingston's alone? Where is your assistant?"

Shauna's interest was piqued too. "Yeah, when do I get to meet Ryder?"

"Never," Lola said quickly to cut her off and turned back to me. "He didn't tell me he had the day off."

"He didn't but he wasn't in a great mood. So when friends asked him to go swimming at the beach, I told him to go."

It was easy to see by her expression that she was slightly upset about Ryder not mentioning his swim plans.

Lola quickly swept some invisible dust off the counter. "Good for him. I hope he has fun," she said in a tone that didn't match the words. I, of course, kept that observation to myself, but Shauna laughed about it.

"It doesn't sound like you want him to have fun at all," Shauna mused. "It seems like you're kind of mad he went without you."

Lola spun around and scowled at her. "What I'm mad about is the splinters of glass still on the floor. Go inside the office closet. There's a portable vacuum on the shelf. Bring it out here and pick up every tiny piece so Bloomer doesn't hurt himself."

Shauna realized, too late, her mistake. She looked a bit twitchy and nervous as she headed off with her broom. Lola snatched the broom from her hands before she got two steps. "I'll keep sweeping and pick up all the other pieces you missed."

Shauna walked dejectedly to the office.

"Nice meeting you, Shauna," I called.

A smile returned to her face as she looked back. "You too. Have fun at the movies." She disappeared around the corner.

I favored Lola with my own scowl. "Meanie. She just said she's getting over anxiety issues."

Lola waved it off. "Please, the kid was born anxious."

I shook my head. "All right. Let her know if she needs anything I'll be glad to help. When do you leave?"

"Tomorrow morning."

"So soon?" I walked around to her side of the counter. A chunk of glass crunched beneath my sandal. "Oops, think I found a piece only now it's a bunch of pieces." I reached over and hugged her. "Have a safe trip. And remember, I don't want a shirt that says 'my best friend went to France and all I got was this stupid shirt'."

Lola laughed. "I'm insulted that you'd think I was that boring and unoriginal. I'll find you something."

I patted Bloomer once more and headed to the door. I glanced back at her. "You are going to say good-bye to him, right? Otherwise, I might as well give him the whole week off."

Lola nodded. "Yes, we are going to dinner tonight. Have fun at the movies with Mr. Wonderful."

"I plan to."

CHAPTER 5

*H*ammering woke me from an early evening nap. I sat up groggily from my awkward position on the couch. I leaned forward and stretched my arms up to the get the kinks out. My back was sticky and my hair was glued to the perspiration on my forehead.

Once I got home, I went straight to work opening all the windows in the house. It was an unrewarded attempt to cool the place off. After having a smoothie for breakfast and gelato for lunch, my stomach churned for something solid. I'd decided to throw caution to the wind and make a grilled cheese. I could still smell it throughout the house. I was sure I'd be dreaming about grilled cheese in my sleep.

The hammering started again. I walked to the kitchen window. I couldn't see Dash's roof, but there was a tall ladder leaning against the back of the house. He must have decided to move his construction project outside to avoid the stuffy warmth of the house. It sounded like a good idea to me too.

Kingston stared at me from his cage. It seemed he was mad I'd taken him from his air conditioned perch in the shop. Nevermore had barely touched his food before slinking off to the bedroom for another nap. I tossed a few peanuts into Kingston's bowl. That snapped him out of his glowering mood. It was never too hot for peanuts. Or too cold. Or too early. Or too late.

I grabbed a bottle of green tea from the refrigerator and headed out to the porch to drink it. The hammer cracked the thick, still air. I trotted down the steps to get a view of the noisy action next door. Dash had removed a large swath of shingles from his roof. He was replacing the wood with a new sheet of plywood. His white t-shirt was plastered to his tanned skin. He had wrapped a red bandana around his forehead to keep the sweat out of his eyes. He carefully placed a nail at the edge of the wood and gave it three hard blows.

I walked to his front yard and shielded my eyes to watch him. He still hadn't seen me, but his dog, Captain, greeted me with a lazy tail wag before dropping his big head down on his pillow again.

"I used to help my dad build stuff in his garage," I said loudly.

Dash turned around and wiped his forehead with his arm. His white smile flashed from his tanned face. I'd only recently learned that Dash had been the cause of Briggs' divorce. Briggs had married his high school sweetheart at a young age. It turned out to be a heartbreaking mistake. But the mistake was made worse when his best friend, Dashwood Vanhouten, betrayed him. Of course, there was a good dose of betrayal from Olivia, his wife, too but Briggs wasn't able to forgive Dash. I couldn't blame him, only I was in the awkward position of living next door to Dash. And he'd never given me any reason not to like him as a friend. It was something Briggs was working through. I'd decided to give him as much time as he needed. In the meantime, Dash and I were still friends. Just not close friends.

Dash tromped carefully over to the edge of the roof. He grinned down at me. "I don't picture you as the construction type."

"Considering it usually took me thirty or forty swings of the hammer to put in one crooked nail, you're probably right. Did you have a leak?"

He glanced back at the large patch. "Yeah, I've been meaning to get to it. The house was so hot, I decided to move the work outside."

"I figured that's what happened. It's so hot in my house, I feel like I'm shrinking while I sleep. Like a cotton t-shirt in the hot dryer."

Dash laughed and the movement made him slip forward. My heart nearly popped from my chest, but he easily caught himself.

"Think this is why I avoided patching the roof."

"I'll stop distracting you and let you get back to it. Be careful." I headed back to my porch steps and sipped my tea. From my front yard, I could see down to the water. I couldn't see the marina and pier, but the tall tower of the lighthouse was my favorite focal point. Farther out on the horizon, it looked as if a thin layer of gray clouds was forming. As much as I hated foggy mornings that sent my curly hair into a crazy fit, I would gladly walk around with the Shirley Temple hairdo if it meant a drop in temperature. I pulled out my phone and swiped open the weather app. There was no sign of relief.

I put my phone down and picked up my tea. I sucked in a big, choking gulp when Dash's yell startled me. The clamor of a ladder falling to the ground was followed by a thud and a groan.

My heart pounded so hard I could hear it in my ears. I dropped the tea and ran toward Dash's house. Captain was close on my heels as I pushed through the gate into his backyard. I saw the top of the fallen ladder before I found Dash. He was sitting on the ground, rocking back and forth in pain and holding his arm close to his stomach. The tan on his face had faded to an olive green.

I rushed to him and knelt down. "What can I do? How can I help?" I felt lightheaded from worry.

Dash looked down at the arm he held. "I think I broke my collarbone. My shoulder broke my fall. I'm trying not to move my arm because it hurts. I'm feeling sick from the bone break, but I think I'll be all right to drive myself to the hospital if I just rest a few minutes."

"Nonsense. I'll drive you to Mayfield Medical Center. You sit here and gather your bearings. I'll go get my keys." I raced back through the gate and into the house. Kingston stared at me as if I was nuts as I searched frantically for my keys and purse. My phone rang as I ran down the front steps but I ignored it.

I circled back to where Dash had fallen. He'd gotten himself to his feet, but he looked shaky and pale. He held his arm tightly against him. A wave of nausea rolled through me when, for the first time, I noticed that his right shoulder was lower than the left. The deformity proved his prediction about the broken collarbone.

I hurried to his left side. "Here, put your arm around my shoulder and I'll help you to the car." He was still unsteady enough that when his arm draped around me his weight nearly made my knees collapse.

He sucked in a breath and straightened his legs. "Jeez, sorry about that. I'm still out of it. Thanks for your help, Lacey. I can see now that I probably couldn't drive myself."

We walked awkwardly and slowly out of the backyard. "I'm glad to help. Besides, I owe you. I vaguely recall getting stuck in that stupid old mansion, in the dark, no less, and you came to my rescue. And then there was that time I was trying to get my keys from my silly bird on top of the roof and you caught me. So consider this a debt paid by a friend." Ungainly pair that we were we managed to reach my car.

His face had regained some of its natural color but he was still in a good deal of pain. It took him a minute to lower his large frame into my tiny car. He filled up the front seat and barely had enough room for his long legs.

He carefully pulled the seatbelt across with his left arm while I climbed into the driver's seat and started the motor. My racing heart was finally returning to its normal pace. The surge of adrenaline I'd experienced when I heard Dash fall was starting to subside. Considering it was a fall from a roof, it could have been far worse. A broken collarbone was painful and inconvenient but manageable.

Dash leaned his head back and closed his eyes. "I'm so stupid. And cheap. I should have just called a roofer."

"Probably. You could have been badly hurt, Dash."

"Yeah." He lifted his head and opened his eyes. "As my shoes stuttered down the shingles like a pair of rusty roller skates, my mind went right to survival mode. I grabbed for the ladder but lost my grip and it fell away. Then I was at that point of no return when I knew some part of my body was going to slam cement. I've broken my ankle before and it was not fun, so I sort of twisted around to tuck and roll out of it." He laughed weakly, then winced at the pain the movement caused. "You know, like the stunt people jumping from a moving train. But I didn't get fully into the roll and landed right on my shoulder."

It was my turn to wince. "Sounds painful but it seems quick thinking kept you from being more gravely injured."

"It seems that way." He rested back again with a sigh. "I've got so much work to do down at the marina. This is going to set me back big time."

I felt truly sorry for him.

The emergency entrance was at the back of the hospital. I pulled into one of the many empty parking spots. "Looks like it's not very crowded, which is a good thing. I suppose most people are inside, sitting by their air conditioners and fans."

"Are you saying there was only one person silly enough to climb on his roof tonight?"

"Those are your words. Not mine." I smiled and patted his good shoulder. "Really, I'm just glad it's not worse, Dash."

"Me too." He went to reach for the door and remembered too late that moving his arm was a bad idea. He gritted his teeth at the pain.

"Let me be the chivalrous one and get that door for you." I opened my door. "Just sit tight."

I scurried around to the other side of the car and opened the door. Dash stared up at me with big puppy dog eyes. "I hate being this helpless," he said.

I waved him out with a flourish. "You'll be my strong, helpful neighbor in no time once the doctors patch you up. Do you have your wallet and insurance card?"

He patted his back pocket. "Yep. Maybe I should have landed on my bottom. My wallet is so stuffed with old receipts and useless junk, it might have padded my fall. Although I've had a broken tailbone before and it hurts like heck."

We headed to the big glass doors of the emergency room. "Broken ankle, broken tailbone. Maybe your parents should have covered you in bubble wrap."

He laughed. "Exactly what my dad suggested after my third trip to the emergency room all in the space of one long, accident prone summer. I was sort of fearless when I was young. Fearless and stupid."

The young woman behind the check-in desk went into a mild state of stunned excitement when she saw her next client. Even with a crooked shoulder and a grimace on his face, Dash caused a splash. My phone rang as Dash took a seat at the woman's window.

I leaned over. "I'll just be outside taking this phone call."

Dash glanced up at me. "You can go, Lacey. I'll figure out a way to get home. This could take awhile." His suggestion seemed to perk the ears of the woman checking him in. Something told me he could easily find a ride home from one of several willing hospital workers, but I had no intention of abandoning him.

"My pets are fed and it's much cooler in the hospital than my house. I don't mind waiting." I searched blindly through my purse and found my phone. It was Briggs.

"Hello."

"Hi, did you get my message?"

I thought back to the few harried moments at home. My phone had rung but I was in too much of a state of alarm to answer it. "No, I didn't. I'm at the hospital." I realized instantly that saying those four words over the phone was not the best way to start a conversation. I could hear a short gasp come from his side.

"What's happened? Are you all right? I'll be right there," he shot out his side of the conversation like bullets, and I couldn't get a word in edgewise.

The big doors slid open. I left behind the cool, antiseptic smelling hospital and reentered the sticky, hot night air. The stark difference in temperature was like a gentle slap in the face. "James," I said abruptly. "I'm fine. Dash fell off his roof and got hurt. I drove him to the Mayfield Hospital."

"Couldn't he have just called a friend or an ambulance?"

"James," I snapped harshly. "Shouldn't your next question have been was he hurt badly? You are a police officer, after all. You need to worry about the well being of all your citizens. Even Dash." I stopped my lecture and immediately repeated it in my head, wondering if I sounded far too angry. But in truth, I was angry.

"You told me you drove him so it was easy to deduce that he wasn't hurt badly. I'm a police officer, after all." He threw my admonishing words back at me and they stung. The coolness of his tone assured me my lecture had hit a nerve. (My driving Dash to the hospital had probably already struck a big one too.) It was our

38

first spat since we'd decided to take our relationship past the friendship stage and I didn't like it much.

My voice wavered a little as I spoke into the phone. The fright of the evening had left me more shaken than I realized. What I needed from Briggs was support, not irritation. I decided to continue on letting him know that his dislike for Dash was not going to get in my way. "I should get back inside in case Dash needs me to fill out some paperwork."

"Lacey," he said in a placating tone, but I wasn't having it. I'd done nothing wrong to have him question anything about the evening.

"Really, James, I think it's better if we just end the call for now."

"Yes, you should hurry back in to him in case he needs you." So much sarcasm came with his statement it made my phone feel heavy in my hand.

"Fine, I will," I said sharply and hung up. I blinked the ache from my eyes. This was not a time for tears. All I'd done was something any normal person with a conscience and half a heart would have done. I reached the glass doors and stomped hard on the cement to open them.

Dash was still sitting at the check-in window. Something told me the young woman with the nice smile behind the window was taking just a little longer than usual to check in the patient. It might end up being a very long night. Now I was feeling extra hot under the collar, and it had nothing to do with the heat wave.

I marched back into the hospital and up to the window. Dash glanced casually up at me, then his face snapped toward me again. "Anything wrong? You look upset."

I bit my lip to keep the rant welling up inside of me tucked away. I needed Lola not Dash, but she was out to dinner with Ryder. I'd just have to go home and vent to Nevermore. He tended to be a good listener, even if he was thin on advice.

I felt my forced smile in my cheeks. "Everything is fine. Did you need me to fill out any paperwork?"

Dash grinned back at the young woman behind the window. She had lovely long eyelashes and a small overbite that made her extra cute. "Miss Strathmore was nice enough to fill in the paperwork. All I had to do was scribble a signature with my left hand." Dash turned a concerned expression up toward me again. "Are you sure you're all right?" His face blanched. "Wait, I'll bet I can guess who the call was from. Is he mad that you brought me here?"

I shook my head. I'd made a point of never discussing Briggs with Dash. "It's fine." I heard my own words echo back to me off the window. "Wait. No it's not. I'll be right back." I turned on my heels, pulled out my phone and dialed Briggs.

I considered the possibility that he wouldn't answer but he picked up on the first ring. "I'm sorry, Lacey," he said as I simultaneously barked, "you listen here, James Briggs," into the phone.

I skated right past his brief apology. I needed to get out my thoughts before I lost them. "Dash fell from his roof. Let that scenario percolate for a second, Detective Briggs. He was visibly shaken and frankly, so was I. If you'd prefer the kind of heartless woman who could just walk away from a friend in need, and yes, I said friend, then maybe I'm not the woman you want to be with. What happened between you two is on your plate not mine. It's certainly changed my opinion of Dash, but I wasn't about to let him sit alone in his yard in pain and shock." I stopped and took a shuddering breath. I was on the verge of tears, but I'd managed to hold them back. He was silent on the other side so I continued. "Just what kind of person would I be if I'd left Dash on his own after he'd fallen from the roof?"

"You're right, Lacey. I'm sitting here stewing in my own vat of shame right now. You did the right thing. I know exactly what kind of person you are. That's why I adore you."

His last words made the sob I'd been holding back burst out. I covered my mouth to stifle the next one.

"Are you crying?"

"No," I said through a sob. I wiped my eyes. "I'm still shaken from the whole thing. I didn't know what I'd find when I rushed into his yard."

"How is he doing?" his question seemed genuine and that made my throat tighten a bit more.

I swallowed back the lump. "He'll be fine. But he broke his right shoulder so he's going to be one armed for awhile. I'm sorry I got so snippy with you, but you made me feel guilty for something that I shouldn't have felt guilty about."

"Yes, I did. I put the total blame on my ego and my ignorance. I called earlier to see if you wanted to come over and watch some television. The air conditioner in my house works again. But you're busy tonight, so I'll see you tomorrow."

I glanced back in through the doors. Dash was being taken into a room.

"Just so you know, James, I would much rather be watching television with you in your air conditioned house than sitting in a hospital emergency room."

"That's good to hear. I think. See you tomorrow, Lacey."

"Yep and don't forget our movie date."

"I won't. Good night."

"Good night." I hung up and sighed with relief. The evening had started so simply with a grilled cheese and nap and had somehow ended up an emotional roller coaster ride. But it seemed the ride had ended and I'd survived.

CHAPTER 6

he outside temperature had cooled overnight enough to allow me to cook up an omelet for my convalescing neighbor. I dropped some bread into the toaster to go along with it.

There was always far more waiting than doctoring during an emergency room visit, and the night before had been no different. After waiting an hour for the x-rays to be analyzed, the emergency room doctor called in an orthopedic specialist. That took another hour and the consult, another hour after that. In the end, it was decided to immobilize Dash's arm and let the shoulder heal on its own. Fortunately, it had broken just the right way that the bones could easily fuse back together without the help of a titanium plate. As long as Dash stayed off roofs and ladders for awhile. He was relieved not to have to go through surgery, but he wasn't thrilled about having his arm strapped to his body.

We'd gotten home just before midnight. Dash trudged into his house feeling pretty good on the pain medicine they gave him, and I headed home and dropped right into bed. The alarm went off at seven, but it felt like I'd just fallen asleep. After the third hit on the snooze button, Nevermore took matters into his own paws and started batting at my chin to wake me. Kingston had joined in with a low, grumpy caw from under the sheet on his cage.

I filled a travel cup with fresh coffee and covered the breakfast plate with cellophane for the walk next door. Dash and I had exchanged keys long ago in case of emergency, and feeding my neighbor, who couldn't exactly make breakfast for himself, was a semi-emergency at the very least.

Dash was sitting on the couch with Captain at his feet when I knocked and let myself in. He took a deep whiff. "Breakfast?"

"Cheese omelet, buttered toast and coffee." I held up the cup.

"You win for neighbor of the year, my friend. I was just thinking about pouring myself a bowl of cereal, but it all sounded like too much effort with one hand."

I placed the food on his kitchen table. He was always working on something in the house. I had yet to see it fully furnished or not in some state of disarray. The floor in the kitchen had been stripped down to the subfloor and half of the cabinet doors were off.

"You'll have to excuse the mess," he called as I looked in remaining drawers for a fork. "I'm under construction . . . still. Sometimes it feels like I'll never be finished. And when I do get something done, another problem pops up. I know they sell cars that are called lemons, but I think I bought a lemon of a house."

"Not at all." I handed him the fork. "You're just in a dark mood because you're strapped down like a mummy on one side. The right side and most important side too. Now I'm going to attempt the bike ride to work because I'm feeling like a wimp. Elsie probably ran five miles and baked two hundred treats by now. My accomplishments for the morning are an omelet, toast and a pot of coffee."

"Don't forget earning the neighbor of the year award."

"Oh, right. There is that." I laughed. "It seems like you're feeling a little better. That's good." I headed toward the door.

"Lacey," he said quietly. "I'm sorry if I caused any problems between you and Briggs last night."

I smiled at him. "Everything is smoothed out. Enjoy your day off. I guess *enjoy* might be too strong of a word. Try and get some rest."

He held up his fork. "Thanks for the breakfast."

I walked out and headed across to my garage. The sun had only been fully up for an hour and a half but it was already hard at work baking the town below. Still, I was determined to ride to the shop.

I rolled the bike out and ran inside to get my backpack and keys. I stopped in front of Kingston's cage. He stared back at me. "What do you say? Want to fly to town today?"

He stood up from his perch. But instead of hopping off to walk out the door of his cage, he turned around. His tail feathers spread out for a second, then he relaxed back into a crouched position.

"Guess you made that pretty clear. And rather rudely at that," I added.

It was still early enough in the day that the heat was not yet overwhelming. I climbed perkily onto my bike. (Of course the trip to town was mostly downhill, which made it far less daunting.) The cotton candy pink Crape Myrtle blossoms had begun to shed, carpeting the street with pastel popcorn. The early morning bike ride refreshed me after my long, stressful evening.

As I pedaled past Graystone Church, I noticed the bright red doors were propped open. Welcoming in the cool morning air, no doubt. The old church, like the Pickford Lighthouse, was one of those charming relics from a time long past. The pale yellow storm shutters were open wide, exposing the stained glass window panes running along the side of the church. The lone, slate covered steeple stood proud over the earthy brown shingles covering the exterior of the church. In the bright summer sunlight, it looked

44

quaint and inviting. But I knew, too well, on a gloomy, stormy night with only a hollow moon and the glow through the windows to light the church and its accompanying graveyard, it could look creepy.

The northernmost half of the cemetery was covered in modern, smoothly carved granite headstones. Behind the plot of sleek, polished headstones were the gravestones from Port Danby's past. Some of the markers were crudely carved crosses and arched stones that jutted up in no particular order and not necessarily perpendicular to the earth. Further back were the more stately, skillfully carved headstones, statues and family plots of the wealthier end of society, including the plot of the Hawksworth family.

I took a small detour onto Graystone Church Way just for fun. Briggs had brought up the family murder mystery. I realized I'd been somewhat neglectful of my self-assigned task. Aside from the account ledger, I'd discovered a letter from someone referred to as "Button". The letter recipient was "Teddy". There was no way to misconstrue the content of the letter. It was a poetically written love letter. Button had even included a sprig of dried lavender, which had stayed perfectly preserved in the folded parchment .

I parked my bike and walked over the lumpy grass leading to the older half of the graveyard. The Hawksworth family plot was by far the most majestic. It was surrounded by a black wrought iron fence. Two white columns supported a Greek style portico that framed the massive family headstone. Hawksworth was carved in curly fancy script into the stone. Each of the murdered family members, Bertram, Jill and their three children had their own marker. The mystery that still remained was the unmarked grave right next to Cynthia, the youngest. A gray stone sat perched in front of a stretch of grass but there was no name carved into it. I'd considered the possibility that Bertram had a favorite hunting dog or the family had a beloved cat that they'd buried in the family plot. But then why bother going through the expense of honoring the pet without adding a name to the stone. And it did seem that burying a pet in a human cemetery might have been considered disrespectful or in poor taste. Even from the richest, most influential family in town.

I turned back and headed toward the church. A pair of pigeons had landed on the top step. It seemed they were considering a quick trip inside to look for crumbs. I decided to join them. Only *I* was looking for different crumbs.

The two pigeons were not happy to have me walk through and disrupt their plans. They fluttered off toward the trees. They would have been disappointed anyhow. The small chapel was spotless. There were no crumbs of food in sight.

Bright sun streaked through the colorful window panes casting a rainbow of shapes and colors on the ivory painted walls. The end of the narrow corridor leading into the chapel had the crumbs I was hoping to find. They had nothing to do with baked goods. Someone had neatly arranged a six by four array of framed pictures that showed the church at various stages in time. A small brass plaque attached to each picture frame provided the date of the photo. According to the first photo, one dated June 17, 1899, the church had no steeple or shutters. Old railroad ties were used as steps up to the front stoop. The 1903 picture showed the construction of the steeple and the addition of new front doors. I moved to the next picture. It was dated July 3, 1906, just three months before the Hawksworth murders. The picture was taken at an angle that showed the cemetery. Naturally, there were far fewer headstones and statues at that time. The new section of cemetery was still just a stretch of grass. I pulled my glasses out from my backpack and pushed them on to get a better look at the grainy image.

The wrought iron fence that bordered the Hawksworth family plot was already standing but there were no headstones yet. They were still three months away. It seemed Bertram Hawksworth had purchased the family plot in preparation for the future. But did he know that bleak future was just a few months away? Was it possible that, like the investigators concluded, Bertram Hawksworth had killed his family? Or was he just a man who liked to be prepared for anything? Maybe he wanted to make sure his family had an eventual resting place in Port Danby.

As I pulled my gaze away, my eyes caught something in the picture. I had to press my face closer, near enough that my glasses tapped the frame on the picture. The Hawksworth family plot was empty except for one gravestone, the unmarked stone. It was there. Someone had been buried in the family plot months before the October murder, and whoever that person was, their name was kept secret. It was entirely possible Bertram and Jill had planned to have the stone carved, maybe with some intricate, unique design like the train etched into William's headstone, but their own unforeseen demise stopped those plans.

A woman who had been polishing the pews in the church walked toward the corridor. She was slightly hunched over and her cheeks were pink from work. "Can I help you, dear?" she asked. Her voice trembled as much as her fingers holding the dusting cloth.

"No, I was just perusing these old pictures. It's wonderful seeing the historical timeline of Graystone Church in pictures." I turned away from the photos and took off my glasses. Her blue eyes were cloudy with age. I wondered how many times she'd polished the church pews in her lifetime.

"My Great Aunt Mary started that photo collection back in 1899." She lifted a gnarled finger toward the first frame. "My Uncle Thomas took this picture."

I smiled up at the photo. It was fairly good quality and amazingly clear for such an old image. "He was talented." I turned back to her. "I was wondering about something. Maybe you can help me. I took a walk around the cemetery grounds to look at the old statues and headstones. I noticed that one of the gravestones in the Hawksworth family plot is blank. No name or date mentioned. I saw a grave marker for each of the children. Do you know who is buried there?"

The pillow of gray hair piled on her head wobbled as she shook her head. "Such a tragedy, isn't it? It's terrible to think that a man could murder his own family in cold blood. And three children too." She shook her head again.

"Yes, it is very sad," I noted quickly. "But the unmarked grave, do you know who it is? Or perhaps there are some church records?"

The woman rubbed her chin. "Unmarked grave? I'm not sure." She chuckled weakly. "I rarely walk out there anymore. The grass is so uneven, I can't get across it without my cane. But I think that it's always been there."

"Yes." I pointed up to the picture. "I can see it here. It was there before the family was murdered."

Her gray hair wobbled again. "So terrible. What would drive a man to kill his own children? I just don't know what the world is coming to," she said once again, adding a head shake to punctuate the end of her comments.

It was hard not to smile at her 'what is the world coming to' comment since this particular crime happened more than a century ago.

"Well, thank you for your help. I should get to work. I enjoyed our chat."

She waved her dust cloth as I turned to leave. "Anytime, dear."

CHAPTER 7

*R*yder swept the same spot on the floor for a good five minutes before I decided to clear my throat loudly to let him know it was probably overkill. It shook him out of his sweeping trance.

I poked the last orange rose into a special order birthday bouquet and stepped back to admire my handiwork. "I think we should use these orange roses more. I know most people gravitate toward the traditional red, pink and white, but these orange roses are so vibrant. They make me happy just looking at them." I picked up an extra rose and walked it over to Ryder. "Here. Have a happiness rose. I'm tired of your frown."

He took hold of the rose and twirled the stem in his fingers. "Actually, the orange rose came from an experimental cross breeding of red and yellow species. When you give one, it's suppose to signify love that began as friendship."

I smiled up at him. "Or it could just mean happiness. That's the interpretation I'm sticking with. Do you want to go to lunch early? You look hungry."

"That's not hunger you're seeing," he said mournfully.

"All right, chat time." I took the broom from his hand and waved him toward one of the stools. "Sit and I will give you the miniscule insight I have from being both your friend and Lola's."

Ryder seemed hesitant about the upcoming conversation, but he swung his long leg over the stool and settled on top of it. His glum expression and surrendered posture were not exactly encouraging but I forged ahead.

I sat on the second stool and faced him. "First of all, and I say this not as a friend to either of you but as a woman. There is nothing less attractive than a mopey man. And you, my friend, are making Eeyore, Pooh's depressed, gloomy, pessimistic donkey friend, look exuberant. So stop or I'm going to pin a tail on you. If you want to keep Lola's interest, you have to wear a little less emotion on your sleeve and be just a touch more aloof. She'll be back soon, and I know she'll be thinking about you while she's away."

"You're right about all of this but it's hard. I've never felt this way about anyone before."

I reached over and patted his arm. "Don't forget, you have big plans to travel the world to study plants in other regions. I'm sure Lola is keeping that in the back of her mind. She figures you're going to walk away from her someday. She's keeping her feet on the ground about this whole thing because of your future plans."

Ryder nodded. "I know. I keep asking myself if I'm going to be able to go through with them now."

"You have to. If you change your lifelong dream because of Lola, you'll lose her anyway. She'll never forgive herself if she keeps you from your horticulture adventure. That's still a year or two off, right?" I asked in a moment of selfishness. I dreaded the thought of trying to replace Ryder.

"Two years is the plan. And you're right. I'm going to stick to it."

He stood from the stool. "And I'm done with moping and frowning."

I jumped down from my stool too. "Good for you." I swept my hands back and forth. "My work here is done. Not the florist work. The friendly advice stuff." I circled back around to the birthday bouquet I'd been working on.

"Hey, boss," Ryder said as he picked up the broom. "Thanks for noticin' me," he said in an amazingly accurate Eeyore voice.

"Oh my gosh, you can do imitations." I tilted my head side to side. "Of course you can. You can do everything." I pointed at him. "And don't you forget that. Now, since it's such a quiet day—" Right then a loud rumbling sound shook the shop enough to rattle the front window and topple a few empty vases. I instinctively grabbed for the edge of the island counter. Ryder steadied himself too.

"Was that an earthquake?" I asked. My heart thumped loudly just as it had the night before when Dash fell off the ladder.

Ryder hurried to the window and peered out. "If it was, then it seemed to happen only beneath our shop. Everything looks peaceful and normal out there."

"The noise came from Les's side of the sidewalk. I think I'll walk over and make sure he's all right." I stepped outside and walked next door to Lester's coffee shop. I quickly found the source of the earthquake. Les was scooting around picking up his pub style bar stools from the sidewalk. He was muttering angrily to himself as he retrieved all his runaway furniture.

I glanced back toward the outer wall of my shop and took several shocked steps back. Les had set up a massive, industrial sized fan to cool off his sitting area. The diameter of the fan was a good six feet across and the blades were as big as airplane propellers.

Les spotted me standing with my mouth dropped open and my eyes popping from my head. "Lacey," he blurted, "did I cause any damage to your shop?" His face was red and it wasn't just from the heat or the sunny yellow and orange print on his Hawaiian shirt. He raced over to me. "Is everything all right?"

I finally pulled myself from my moment of shock. "Everything is fine, Les, but how are you?" He knew exactly what I was asking and answered accordingly.

"Considering I nearly blew away my furniture and the entire coffee shop with the large fan I borrowed, it seems I might be ready for the funny farm." I followed him to the other fallen furniture and helped him right the stools. He looked thoroughly disappointed that his plan was a disaster.

"I have to say, Les, I think those are the kind of fans they use to create hurricanes on movie sets. Something smaller might be more practical."

The heat was too much for him. He sat on the last stool he set upright. "Little handheld fans, that's what Elsie bought for her customers. She's always one step ahead of me in the brains department." He chuckled. "That's what our dad used to tell us too."

I picked up a stool and sat across from him. "I don't see the handheld fans being a big hit on the other side of the shop either. It's just too hot to sit outside. You should focus more on cool drinks like special iced coffees and frappés. That's where you can easily outshine Elsie. It's hard to make a baked good refreshing, but coffee can be perfect on a hot day if it's done up right."

Les pulled a tissue out of his shirt pocket and blotted his forehead. "You know something, you're right. I should go inside and come up with a brilliant new iced drink. One that will pull people off the hot sidewalk and into the shop. Thanks, Lacey. I needed that pep talk."

I wiped my hands back and forth again. "Pep talks seem to be my specialty today so I'm glad to help. Maybe I should walk up and down the street and pop into each shop to see if anyone else needs a little cheery, sage advice from the local florist." I stood up to leave.

"If you do go out on the Lacey Pinkerton advice tour, be sure to stop in the bakery and keep my sister occupied for an hour. I need to have the guy who rented me this fan come and pick it up before she sees it. She'll never let me live it down. Knowing Elsie, she'll have a picture of the fan carved into my headstone just for fun."

I laughed and stopped in front of the fan for a second. "I think I could use this thing in fall when all the leaves drop in my front yard. It would save me a lot of time raking. Take care, Les, and if you need someone to sample your new coffee frappés, I'm your gal."

CHAPTER 8

I was still on the Lacey Pinkerton super helper tour when I decided to fix Dash a sandwich for dinner. It was too hot in my house to cook anything and a sandwich seemed a little underwhelming for a dinner offer, but it was better than nothing.

I headed across his front yard in my favorite spaghetti strap sundress. It had taken me a good half hour to decide if the theater would be too hot or too cold, as they often are. But after several brutal days of high temperatures, I settled on the idea that if it was too cold that would be a good thing

I knocked and was about to pull out my key when Dash opened the door. He'd removed the sling that kept his arm pasted to his body.

"Uh oh, are you ignoring doctor's orders?" I slipped past him with the sandwich. "I made you a submarine sandwich, but I won't be insulted if you don't eat it tonight. Maybe you've already had dinner."

Dash followed me as I headed to the kitchen with the sandwich. "Actually, a friend is supposed to be bringing over some burgers."

"I see." I'd so easily declared that I wouldn't be insulted and then was instantly insulted. Or maybe it was disappointment. After my heart to heart with Ryder and my pep talk with Les, I was two for two on my helper tour. But it seemed tonight's good deed was a bust. "Well, I'll put the sandwich in the refrigerator for tomorrow's lunch."

"Or a midnight snack." He reached up with his free hand and raked his fingers through his thick head of hair.

I looked pointedly at his right arm. "Aren't you supposed to have that arm immobile?"

He looked down at it. "It is. I'm not using it. Actually, that's a lie. Earlier, I knocked my soda can off the counter. My first instinct was to catch it." He scrunched up his face to let me know that didn't end well.

I scrunched along with him. "You used your right arm?"

"It shot right out. Long story short, I missed the can and spent an hour waiting for the pain to subside. But that restrictive splint was driving me nuts. When I was little, my mom used to make me wear this ugly, tight turtleneck to holiday dinners. No matter how much I stretched that darn turtleneck out my head always got stuck in it. I'd panic and thrash until my head popped free. That splint was bringing back that same claustrophobia induced panic attack."

I raised my brow at him. "Don't you spend half your work day jammed inside engine compartments?"

"Yeah, I know, it's crazy. But when I'm inside the engine compartments, I can move both arms freely." Dash lifted his face and glanced out his front window. "Looks like Briggs just pulled into your driveway."

"He's early. I should get going then. Enjoy burgers with your friend." I headed to the door and snuck a smiling peek back at him.

"By any chance, does this friend wear stylish vintage clothes and a new hair color every week?"

His mouth shifted side to side to stop a grin. "It's possible. Did you tell Kate about my shoulder?"

"Nope, wasn't me. But you know how word gets around in this town."

"Do I ever. Anyhow, she called and asked if she could come by with some food. I hesitated at first."

"Why is that?"

He tilted his head. "Do you really need to ask? Have fun tonight with Detective Grump."

I rolled my eyes. "And you have a good time with Miss Persistent. Actually, I take that back. Shame on me for saying it. And it is very nice of Kate to bring you dinner." I opened the door. "See you later."

Briggs was just climbing out of his car when I stepped out onto Dash's front porch. I knew darn well that my exit from my neighbor's house was not going to go over well. I steeled myself for his reaction. (Although, the way Briggs looked in his black t-shirt and jeans was not helping my resolve.)

His brown eyes glittered with a touch of something that wasn't outright anger but it wasn't a 'hello how are you' either.

I jumped right into my very acceptable explanation. I flicked my thumb back over my shoulder toward Dash's house. "I was just taking him a sandwich. He isn't supposed to used his right arm and that makes food prep kind of difficult." Naturally, Kate Yardley pulled up right then in her sporty little convertible and her new blonde hair color to throw some water on my explanation. She barely had time to smile our direction in her hurry to get the burgers up to the house.

I turned back to Briggs who had crossed his arms, a gesture that showed off his nice biceps. "Seems Vanhouten is extra hungry from this broken arm."

"Shoulder," I corrected. "It's his shoulder and you know it always takes extra calories to heal from an injury. I'm ready. I'll just check on the pets and get my purse." I continued toward the house but didn't hear Briggs' footsteps following. I stopped and looked back at him. As it turned out, black was the perfect color for brooding. "James?" I asked tentatively.

His mouth was set in a firm line. I could let the whole thing devolve into an argument about Dash, but I'd had about enough of those inane squabbles. "I'll just wait out here," he said quietly.

I climbed the steps to the house feeling less excited about the evening than ten minutes earlier. The flouncy green skirt of my sundress swung around my legs as I rushed around refilling Nevermore's and Kingston's water bowls. I'd put on my favorite dress. I'd even put on a touch of lipstick and the only thing on Briggs' mind was my visit to Dash. It was to say the least, disheartening. But I was determined to get the night back on track. I grabbed my purse and skittered down the steps in my sandals.

Briggs circled around to the passenger side of the car and opened the door when I reached him. He paused and gazed at the dress for a long moment and a faint smile appeared. "You look nice, Lacey."

I was stunned and pleased by the compliment. With any luck, the night had just shifted back to the positive side. "Thank you. My mom always complains that I don't wear dresses enough. I thought Casablanca was just the right movie for it."

"Good choice." He waved me into the car.

He climbed into the driver's seat.

"When are we going to take that motorcycle ride?" I asked. He'd promised several times to take me for a ride on his motorcycle but we'd never firmed up any plans. I'd been looking forward to it.

He backed out of the driveway. "We could go back and get it now, but I think you might regret your fashion choice. And frankly, if I have to choose between my bike and that dress right now, I choose that dress."

My face warmed enough at his comment that I turned toward the window to hide the blush. "You sir, are a scoundrel." I turned back to him. "Is that from Casablanca?"

His longish hair rubbed along the collar of his t-shirt as he shook his head once. "I don't think so. I can't think of any famous movie with that quote, so maybe we can just credit Lacey Pinkerton with that line. And thank you, by the way. It's a first for me, being called a scoundrel. Since I have to spend every day as a law abiding, polite, by-the-book detective, I kind of like the sound of it."

I laughed. "Glad I could boost that side of your ego for a change." It seemed the moment of tension brought about by my untimely exit from Dash's house had vanished. I considered it a win. Maybe we were finally getting past that hill.

"By the way," he reached forward and turned the radio down a notch. "Just by coincidence, Ronald Samuels walked into the police station today to lodge a complaint against Connie Wilkerson."

I blinked at him, confused and waiting for more. "Are these people I should know?" I recognized the names as soon as I asked it. "Right, the movie theater owners. So much has happened these last few days, I'd already erased those names from my mind."

Briggs headed toward the neighboring town of Mayfield. "Really? What happened?"

I shrugged. "I've just been putting out a few fires here and there. Lola left to France this morning. Ryder was feeling glum about it, but I gave him a talking to and he cheered up. Then in an attempt to outdo Elsie and her tiny handheld fans, Les set up a massive industrial fan in his outdoor seating area."

A laugh shot from his mouth. "Massive?"

"Yes, I'm talking blades that were longer than my arm span.

Ryder and I were working and all of a sudden the shop shook and the windows rattled. Scared the dickens out of us."

"The dickens," he repeated. "Never had dickens scared out of me but go on. Did the fan work?"

"It worked just fine if he was going for the hurricane effect. Poor guy was picking up his scattered pub stools off the sidewalk."

"Good ole Les. So I guess the Great Table War is still raging." He turned toward the theater. Connie Wilkerson's theater was on the corner of Turner Boulevard and Main Street. A giant neon lit moon and star hung over the marquee. It was easy to tell the new construction, the section that had been restored after the fire, because the original building was covered in used brick. The new section had brick too but the weather and elements hadn't given them that nicely aged brick patina. We continued along Turner Boulevard to the Mayfield Four Theater at the end of the block.

"You never finished your story," I said. "What was the complaint from Ronald Samuels?"

"Samuels came stomping in, fist's balled, grumbling about being wronged by *'that woman'*."

I covered my mouth to stifle a laugh. "That woman? He actually used that phrase?"

Briggs nodded. "He did indeed. Apparently someone poured salt into his soda machine. Something he didn't notice until movie goers started spitting soda out all over the theater. It took all day for his crew to clean up the mess and the machine had to be drained and cleaned. 'Big profit loss' he grumbled over and over again. By the way, he is not one of those people you'd go out of your way to invite to a summer barbecue or birthday party. Something tells me he's grumpy, salty soda or not."

"See, that's what I was telling you. Trinity, the girl who works for him had nothing but complaints about the man. So he thought Connie Wilkerson from the Starlight Movie Theater was the culprit? Wouldn't he have seen her standing in his theater with her carton of salt?"

"He thinks she paid someone to sabotage the machine." He pulled into the theater parking lot. It was only mildly crowded. A few people had dressed in forties style clothing for the occasion. There were more than a few fedoras but no one bothered with a trench coat in this heat. "I wrote down the complaint and told him I'd talk to Connie."

"It seems the two Mayfield theaters are locked in a bit of drama." I reached for the door handle. "As long as no one salted the lemon-lime slush machine. I've got my heart set on one."

CHAPTER 9

"Two tickets for Casablanca," Briggs said to the woman behind the counter. Her nametag said Sally Applegate and below in tiny silver print were the words 'assistant manager'. Sally seemed to be the artsy type with big hoop earrings, a gauzy, brightly colored shirt and several handwoven bracelets on her wrist. Trinity had mentioned that Sally was the creative mind behind the vintage movie night only Mr. Samuels rarely acknowledged her hard work. Coincidentally, Lola's cousin, Shauna, knew her from her anxiety group.

Sally smiled smoothly at Briggs and gave him a quick appreciative once over. (Couldn't really blame her. That black t-shirt was really working for him.) I certainly didn't see any anxiety or nerves from the woman behind the ticket window.

"I'm thinking popcorn with my lemon-lime slush. It's always important to balance salty with sweet and sour," I added as we handed off our tickets to a young guy with a mass of wavy blonde hair shoved under his red usher hat. His sunburned nose nearly matched the red of the uniform. It took me a second to reconcile the face with the picture Trinity had shown me in the flower shop. This was her boyfriend, Justin. I'd never been to the Mayfield Four theater but it seemed I already knew half the staff.

"Second theater on the right," Justin muttered quickly as he handed back our stubs.

We stepped into the cavernous lobby of theater. Stairs on each side led up to a balcony area on the second floor. The wall to the left of the long treat counter was lined with three noisy, neon colored video games and a large soda machine, apparently the soda machine that was tainted with salt. The right side of the vast, two story room was decorated with exotic glass lanterns and tall baskets of ferns. A richly carved Moroccan table and chairs had been roped off in the center of the display. My guess was that they were just for ambience and not a place for oily popcorn fingers. Colorful silk scarves were draped around the chairs and tables and someone had rolled in an old piano. There was a handwritten sign sitting on top of the piano that said, 'Do Not Touch'. A life-size cardboard cutout of Humphrey Bogart was propped up next to the piano. A large banner boasting some of the more famous quotes from the movie had been pinned to the wall.

Briggs and I stood for a second to take it all in. "Impressive," Briggs noted.

"Trinity"—I motioned toward the candy counter where Trinity was filling a bucket of popcorn for a customer—"She's the sister of my bridal client. She told me that Sally, the woman in the ticket window, was responsible for all the vintage movie night events. However, Mr. Samuels allegedly takes all the credit for himself."

Briggs looked around. "Ah yes, there is the charming Mr. Samuels over there chewing out the boy taking tickets at the door. Doesn't seem like good form to be barking at your employee in front of customers."

Samuels was talking loud enough that we could catch snippets of the angry lecture between gun shots and torpedo blasts on the video games across the way. It had something to do with Justin not taking the time to scrape gum off of seats.

"I had a boss like that when I was in high school," Briggs said. "Mr. Pepper."

I laughed. "Mr. Pepper does not sound like the name of a mean boss. Mr. Hawkeye or Mr. Scrooge or Mr. Blackthorn, yes, but Mr. Pepper makes me want to pop open a can of soda."

"If you'd met the man, you'd understand. He used to chew a nail while he yelled at me for stacking the oil cans wrong in the gas station window."

"How did you manage to stack oil cans wrong?"

"I didn't. I stacked them one on top of the other like any normal person would. Pepper just needed something to complain about. And he found something every day. I finally decided it wasn't worth the thirty bucks a week to work for the man."

"I don't blame you. I think I'd walk too."

Briggs' eyes lifted to the banner. He gave his Bogie impression another whirl. "Of all the gin joints, in all the towns . . ." He started but couldn't keep a straight face. "Guess we should get in line and order that lemon-lime slush." He lowered his voice. "Before someone sabotages it with salt."

I was slightly disappointed he didn't finish the quote. It was always one of my favorite movie lines, and Briggs was just handsome and cool enough to stand in for Bogart. (At least in my biased view.)

Trinity was looking a little miffed at the two women in front of us in line. They couldn't decide between red licorice and malt balls. Her eyes kept drifting to the door where Justin was taking tickets. Mr. Samuels had apparently finished his tirade about gum removal. I didn't see Samuels but he'd definitely soured the mood of his ticket taker. Justin was snatching tickets from hands with a scowl. Not the best form for the person greeting you at the door but then that could be blamed more on the boss than the employee.

The two women finally decided on a bag of gummy worms. Trinity rang them up but was distracted as she counted back their change. A man skirted the line and approached the counter. He looked to be in his thirties. He was a big man, one that might be described as husky or barrel-chested. Three lines between his brows were creased as if he was worried about something. "Tell my dad I'm waiting for him in his office," the man said quickly to Trinity before leaving the counter.

It took a second for the highly distracted Trinity to recognize me. She smiled sweetly at Briggs. "You're the detective in Port Danby." She winked at me. "Nice work."

"Thanks." I smiled sideways at Briggs and passed the wink on to him.

"What can I get for you two?" she asked.

"I think I'm going to try that lemon-lime slush you were raving about." I looked at Briggs.

"I'll try one too. And a large popcorn."

Trinity scooted off to fill our drinks. I glanced around the busy room and spotted Mr. Samuels tromping down the stairs from the balcony, ushering several kids to walk ahead of him. Their heads were dropped as if they'd been caught doing something they shouldn't. He said something to them at the bottom of the stairs and they scurried out the exit. Justin took time out of his ticket collection to skewer his boss with invisible laser beams as Mr. Samuels marched toward the concession stand.

Trinity caught sight of him while she filled the second cup. "Oh, Mr. Samuels, your son is here. He's in his office."

No expression of joy or pleasure followed. In fact, Samuels looked more put out by the visit than anything. I wondered if there was anything that made the man smile. Possibly counting his money like Scrooge on Christmas Eve.

"Fine," he said abruptly. "And bring me one of the lemon-lime slush drinks." He walked toward a small corridor that was marked 'employees only' and disappeared around the corner.

I leaned toward Briggs. "I would not have pegged that grouchy man as the lemon-lime slush type. He seems more like the bitter coffee or sucking on dry lemon type."

"Or gasoline type," Briggs suggested. "He is not exactly warm and welcoming. It's a wonder he has such a successful business."

"I think that the assistant manager can be credited with the theater's popularity more than the manager."

Trinity returned with our slush drinks and popcorn. I glanced around to make sure no one heard.

"You weren't kidding about your boss," I said discretely. "Is he just the manager? Maybe the owner should know about his behavior."

Trinity sighed. "If only that would work. But Mr. Samuels is manager and owner, so we're stuck with him." She handed Briggs his change. "Enjoy the slush and the movie."

I took a quick sip and raised the cup. "Hmm, you were right. This will hit the spot nicely. Thanks."

CHAPTER 10

The ornate sconces running along the side walls of the theater glowed as we walked several steps down and decided on a row that was halfway between the front and back of the theater. The words "Welcome to Vintage Movie Night" were projected across the gigantic screen. About half the seats were filled. Most of the people waiting were either unwrapping snacks or staring at their phones.

After scooting past a few people, Briggs and I decided on two center seats. As he settled into his seat and reached for a handful of popcorn, a woman called his name from the end of the row.

"James? James Briggs? Is that you?"

I glanced to the end of the row. Briggs leaned forward to see who was calling him. Three women around my age were hugging bottles of water and chewing on red licorice whips. The one who had called his name had sleek blonde hair she had tied back with a pink ribbon. She was wearing a vintage Marilyn Monroe style halter dress. One of her friends was wearing what looked like a vintage World War II women's army uniform, complete with the cap pushed down over her dark hair. A third friend was dressed in pedal pusher length blue jeans and a matching denim shirt with sleeves rolled up like Rosie the Riveter. They looked enthusiastic and ready for their vintage movie night. I felt a little like a party pooper for not getting more into the spirit with my twenty-first century dress and sandals.

"Teresa?" Briggs asked. "How have you been? Still living in Chesterton?" He was extra jovial in his reply. I sat back out of the way so he could carry on his conversation.

"Just back in town to visit the parents. You remember Mindy and Helen," she said pointing to her friends.

Briggs nodded. "Yes, good to see you. This is Lacey. She owns the flower shop in Port Danby."

I nodded a hello, then turned to stare at the screen that was still just a stationary set of words welcoming us to the movie night. I was, to say the least, frozen in disappointment and quickly trying to pacify myself. Maybe he just didn't feel it necessary to bring up I was his date or his girlfriend. Maybe he figured it was implied because we were obviously out on a movie date together. Maybe he thought my ownership of the flower shop was the most perti- nent detail to mention in a brief introduction. Yes, those maybes might very well explain the whole thing. Or maybe he just didn't want the women to think he was tied down by a girlfriend.

The rest of their conversation was muted by the analytic thoughts ping ponging through my brain. Briggs finally sat back when the lights dimmed.

I stared straight ahead even though I could feel him looking at the side of my face.

"Friends of yours?" I asked, unnecessarily and with just enough vinegar to surprise even me.

"I went to high school with them." He offered me some popcorn but I shook my head.

"Anything wrong?" he asked. The lights dimmed. A loud

commercial about theater discounts and snacks at the concession stand blasted through the speakers.

"No, this flower shop owner is quite pleased to be sitting here with the famous James Briggs."

He fell silent. My seat shook as he sat back harder than needed. It seemed he was trying to retrace his steps, or, more accurately, his words from the last few minutes. A quiet sound ushered from his mouth, letting me know he'd stumbled upon the critical sentence. "I like to brag about your business, Lacey. I didn't mean to give short shrift in the introduction. Should I tell them you're my girlfriend?"

I turned to him for the first time. "That would be silly. It's fine."

"I could stand up on the chairs and announce to the whole theater that I'm dating the adorable owner of Pink's Flowers and she has me spinning. In fact I'm so dizzy when I think about her, I sometimes find it hard to believe she's my girlfriend."

He got louder with each word. I finally leaned over and kissed him on the mouth to quiet him. We both sat in silence for a moment gazing into each other's eyes just like we were about to see Bogie and Bergman do on the big screen.

I broke into a giddy smile. "Do I really make you dizzy?"

"Trust me, no one has ever made me more dizzy than you, Lacey Pinkerton."

"Good." I sat back and took a handful of popcorn. "I think."

He was still looking at my profile. He cleared his throat. "By the way, that bit of jealousy or whatever that was a second ago, you might think about it if you see me get grumpy when I see you walking out of Dash's house. Or when I call you and find you've driven my mortal enemy to the hospital."

"I don't know if it was jealousy," I said quickly in my defense. "It was more that I felt slighted." I munched on some popcorn and took a sip of slush that was quickly melting into an artificial tasting lemon-lime syrup. It seemed the crushed ice was the star of the drink. I could still feel Briggs' gaze on my face. I turned to him. "All right, there might have been a tiny seed of jealousy. They seemed so excited to see you in their cute forties fashion. Occasionally, I drop back to high school mode. I'm not proud of that fact but it is what it is. It's not easy dating the extremely sought after Detective James Briggs."

His mouth turned up in a crooked, not terribly amused smile.

I grabbed another handful of popcorn. "Fine. I promise to overlook some of your grumpiness when the subject of Dash comes up. As long as you don't overreact."

"I never overreact," he said wryly. "I'm a detective. It's my job not to overreact." He sat forward and glanced back at the projector room up above the auditorium. The commercials had ended. The screen was blank. The lights had been dimmed low but there was no movie.

He sat back. "It seems like the movie should have started by now." Just as he said it, the assistant manager, Sally, appeared in front of the blank screen. "Ladies and gentlemen, there will be a slight delay due to a problem with the projector. Drink refills are on the house while you are waiting. It shouldn't be more than ten minutes. Our team is working on it."

A low mumble of disappointment made its way around the seats. Several people got up with their soda cups to take her up on the free refill offer. Others turned their phones back on and tiny screen lights lit the room up again.

"Do you want a refill on the slush?" Briggs asked.

"No, I think the novelty has worn off. I think I'll go ask for a cup of water. Do you want anything?" I asked.

"No, I'm fine. Do you want me to go?"

"No, thanks, I might stop by the ladies' room too." I scooted past him, avoiding having to slip by his three friends at the end of the row.

I finished up in the restroom and headed out to get the water. A 'temporarily closed' sign was posted outside the men's room. There was a line in front of the men's room on the opposite side of the lobby. It was nice to see the men having to wait for a change, I thought wryly. It seemed the theater was having more than its share of problems this evening. Maybe there was some sort of sabotage in the works, or maybe it was just one of those nights. I'd had plenty of days in the shop when nothing seemed to work out right.

I was in luck. There was no line at the concession stand. Movies in the three other theaters were in full swing. It seemed only our movie was delayed.

The large, square shaped man, who was apparently the owner's son, was standing behind the concession stand. The frown lines between his brows were still noticeable as he shook an alarming amount of parmesan cheese onto his oily popcorn. He shook and swirled the extra large bucket to coat the kernels with the cheese. I supposed when your dad owned the theater, you could help yourself to the popcorn, candy and drinks. My nose picked up the pungent odor of the parmesan a good fifteen feet before I reached the stand.

Trinity was stooped behind the counter refilling the candy shelves. She popped up and saw me coming across the room. I knew exactly what she was going to ask me and I was ready with my answer.

"Was I right? Wasn't that slush the bomb?"

It was definitely feeling like a bomb in the bottom of my stomach. The taste in my mouth reminded me of the time my cousin dared me to eat a spoonful of dry Kool-aid. But I forced a smile. "You were right. Very lemony and limey. But I've still got a lot of popcorn left. Could I get a cup of ice water?"

Her blue eyes rounded. "But the people in the Casablanca film get a free refill." She leaned forward. "Of course, over at the Starlight, every drink can be refilled as often as you like but—" She shot a peek over at the owner's son. He was still trying to coat every kernel of popcorn with cheese and was far too focused on the parmesan to notice our conversation. "Mr. Stingy would never allow it." She crinkled her nose. "In fact, I have to charge you a quarter for the water."

"I need to go back and get my purse then."

Trinity peeked around, spoke quietly and winked at me as if we were about to pull off the greatest heist of all time. "Give it to me on the way out."

"Are you sure?" I whispered. "I don't want to get you in trouble."

"I'm sure." She grabbed a cup to fill with ice and water.

"Dylan." A deep, grumbling voice echoed through the lobby. It was Mr. Samuels. He was holding his lemon-lime slush in one hand and his phone in the other. His bellow had nearly caused his son to drop his popcorn, which would have been a shame since he'd just spent several minutes getting it to cheesy perfection.

Samuels reached the counter. His son pushed the bucket of popcorn casually behind him as if to hide it.

"I've got to head into the projection room," Mr. Samuels barked. "That nimrod can't get the movie started. I don't have time to finish our talk. I think I've said enough on the subject anyhow." Without waiting for Dylan's response, he disappeared into the employees only corridor. He emerged a few moments later. A tool box had replaced the slush drink in his hand. It seemed the projector being used for Casablanca was as vintage as the movie itself.

Trinity handed me the cup of ice water. "Here you go and enjoy the movie. I'm sure they'll get it started soon."

CHAPTER 11

The theater lights had dimmed more and it took me a second to find Briggs in the center row. I scooted past several people and found my seat.

"You're just in time," he said. "Boredom has caused me to stuff myself with popcorn." He leaned the container my direction.

"No, thanks. Just like the slush is only good when it's cold, the popcorn is better when it's hot."

"Very true." He placed the half-filled bucket on the floor beneath his seat. "I can hear some activity up there in the projector room," he noted.

"The manager was called to help while I was at the concession stand. It seems we are going to be seeing the original version, right from the big metal can. I guess they like to keep vintage movie night authentic." I rested back and stretched my feet out.

The lights dimmed again and the movie started. People clapped to show their appreciation. I leaned my head closer to Briggs. The familiar, pleasant scent of his soap wafted toward me. "We humans get excited about the silliest things," I whispered. Right then he took my hand and I pressed my lips together to contain my excitement, proving my theory right.

"This was a great idea," Briggs said quietly.

"Thanks. I figured it was one movie we could both enjoy."

He laced his fingers through mine and squeezed them. My heart skipped a few beats before I finally relaxed enough to watch the movie.

We were an hour into Casablanca when a flashlight lit up the dark. The audience booed and complained. Another round of audible protests rumbled the theater as the penetrating beam of the flashlight rolled over the seats.

"They must be looking for someone," Briggs said.

Through the harsh glow I could make out the silhouette of the figure holding the flashlight. It was Justin. "Maybe someone slipped in without paying. I wouldn't want to face down Mr. Samuels if I'd snuck into his theater."

The light swept over our heads again like the signal beam on a lighthouse. Then it stopped, backed up and fell right on Briggs. He shaded his eyes and looked back at Justin. The usher was making his way down the steps to our row. Wisely, he turned off the light before a small riot erupted.

"Detective Briggs," he whispered loudly over the other people in the row. Naturally, all faces turned our direction. Even people in front turned back to see what was happening.

"James, were you the guy who snuck in?" I snickered behind my hand. "Don't worry, I'll vouch for you. Or we could just make a run for the emergency exit."

Justin had been booed and hissed at but he had no hesitation scooting past the other movie watchers to reach Briggs. "Sir, we need you in the lobby." Now that he was close enough, I could see he was visibly shaken.

Briggs was off duty but he was always ready to jump into law enforcement mode. He got up from his seat without hesitation. No doubt, Justin's rattled appearance prompted him into action without question.

It was certainly not going to be any fun watching the movie without Briggs, so I got up and followed them out. The first thing I noticed was Trinity standing next to the popcorn maker with her hands over her face as if she were crying or scared. Sally Applegate, the assistant manager, was pale and agitated as she tried to clear the lobby and get people back into the theaters. "Please, everyone, the concession stand is closed right now. We need the lobby cleared. We have a medical emergency, and we need to make room for the paramedics."

Sally was doing an admirable job of taking control of things, but it seemed she was just barely holding herself together. Something serious had happened. I could sense it in the air and on the faces of the few employees who were gathered near the employees only corridor. Anxious glances and whispers were being exchanged by the theater workers. The one person I didn't see in the mix was the owner, Mr. Samuels.

I followed behind Briggs as Justin led him across the vast lobby. "Mr. Samuels is sick," he said. "I went in to ask him about who was closing tonight, and I found him on the floor. It might be a heart attack. But he's not moving. Sally has called the ambulance, but she thought you might be able to help."

Sally spotted us as she ushered several people toward the theaters. "Thank you for your help, Detective Briggs," she called, a gesture that caught the attention of the few people still milling about the lobby. If people hadn't yet figured out something terrible had happened, they certainly knew it now.

"Should I go outside and wait for the ambulance?" Justin asked Sally as she neared.

"I'm on my way to do just that." Sally was out the door and away from the frenzy before anyone could stop her. Justin looked stunned and upset at her decision to abandon the scene.

Briggs hurried toward the corridor. "Let us pass," Briggs said as we reached the distraught group. Briggs pushed through and I stayed right behind.

Mr. Samuels' office was camped with wood paneling, no windows and a large desk in the center of the room. Mr. Samuels was lying on his side with his mouth open and his eyes only halfway shut. I knew instantly I was looking at a dead man and naturally, Briggs knew too. But neither of us let on. He crouched down and placed his fingers on Mr. Samuels' neck.

Some of the employees had inched down the hallway to peer into the office. Some were undecided on whether or not they wanted to see what was happening. Others were eager to peer in and find out why Mr. Samuels was on the floor.

Justin stood in the hallway with an upset Trinity tucked under his protective arm. Briggs stood up and held out his arms. "I need all of you to clear the hallway for the medics." The shell-shocked employees backed slowly out of the narrow corridor. Briggs closed the door slightly and returned to where Samuels was lying.

"Is he?" I asked tentatively.

"Yes, he's dead."

CHAPTER 12

*I*t wasn't an easy call on the part of the assistant manager, but once Sally Applegate was briefed on the gravity of the situation and once she'd recovered from the shock, she decided to stop all of the shows, give out three free passes per person and clear the theater. She mentioned that it was a fairly light crowd for the evening which made the decision easier.

I helped hand out passes. It took some time to clear the auditoriums and move curious onlookers toward the parking lot. Unfortunately, the last handful of people witnessed the arrival of the coroner's van as it pulled up in front of the theater. Eyes popped from heads and mouths dropped open at the ominous sight of the vehicle marked 'county coroner'.

"People are already starting to talk," Sally said. Her hand flew to her mouth to stifle a gasp. "We need to tell his son before he hears it from someone else."

"He was here earlier," I said. "Do you know where he might be right now?"

"Possibly visiting his mother in the hospital. She had heart surgery. It was quite serious, but poor Dylan couldn't get Ronald to even pay her a visit. They've been divorced for a few years."

"Do you have his phone number?"

"Yes, I have it in case of emergencies." Her large earrings twirled as she shook her head. "I can't tell him. I just can't." Her voice wavered close to a sob.

I patted her arm. "Of course not. I just need the number. Detective Briggs will talk to him."

"Thank goodness he was here." Sally sniffled once. Something told me she was more shaken than sad about her boss's demise. Death was always shocking and unexpected. But I could have been entirely wrong. It was possible she felt genuinely bereaved by his loss. I was making a judgment based on my own feelings about the man.

"I'll write down his phone number for Detective Briggs," she said.

The theater was empty except for the employees. Justin, Trinity, Sally, two more ushers and the guy in charge of the projector rooms. Briggs had told the entire crew not to leave and to wait in the lobby until he had a chance to talk to them. There was no indication of foul play, but I knew Briggs well. He suspected something was amiss.

I headed into Mr. Samuels' office. Briggs was doing a visual search of the room.

"What are you thinking?" I asked as I reached the man's desk. It was neat and orderly with several file folders stacked perfectly on top of each other and a matching shiny black metal desk set of a pen holder, stapler and paper tray. The only item that didn't belong with the office supplies and paperwork was the red and white striped drink cup. Mr. Samuels had asked Trinity to pour him a slush while he was rushing around doing manager tasks. His son Dylan had been waiting in his office for him in the midst of his busy night, and Mr. Samuels didn't seem thrilled to have to talk to him. I assumed it was because he had too much to do. It did seem like an inopportune time for a family chat. But then Sally mentioned that the ex-Mrs. Samuels was ill in the hospital, so it was possible the conversation required some urgency.

Briggs rested his fingertips against the desk and stared down at the body. "My first instinct would be heart attack. A middle aged man who, from all accounts, is a Type A personality who spends most of his day agitated. Only he never loosened his tie. It's still bound tight near his throat. That might mean nothing at all. It might have been too sudden, but most of the time, if someone is feeling the pain and spasms of a heart attack, they start by unbuttoning top buttons and loosening up clothes to see if that helps."

"That makes sense. From what I've read, it can feel as if there is a huge weight sitting on your chest. I think I'd loosen up my tie and button just to breathe easier."

I plucked a tissue out of the box. "James, may I pick up this cup? It's mostly empty, just the sticky green remnants of the lemon-lime slush. But I'd like to give it a whirl past Samantha." I tapped my nose, one of the few snouts on the planet with its own nickname.

"Yes, please do. Since his mouth is open and slack, I can see that his tongue is stained green from the slush. He was definitely drinking it. Touch the cup near the bottom where someone would be less likely to hold it. That way you won't disturb any prints if they turn out to be important."

I paused before picking up the cup. "Do you think there might be more here than natural causes?"

Briggs shrugged. It was unusual seeing him at a crime scene dressed in a t-shirt and jeans. "Hard to know. I wonder where the coroner is."

"The van pulled up while I was helping Sally hand out free passes. Which reminds me, she's bringing you his son's phone number so you can call him."

He groaned quietly. "I don't look forward to that."

I placed the tissue in my hand and picked the cup up near the bottom. I brought it to my nose expecting to find the same sugary, artificial lime scent of my slush. But another sweetly chemical smell mingled with the lime. It was faint and not something anyone with a normal nose would notice, but I was sure there was something inside the cup besides the last traces of lemon-lime syrup.

Briggs caught my baffled expression. "Something wrong?"

I took another whiff to make sure I wasn't imagining it. "I'd have to smell another cup of the slush to be sure but there's something off about this one. I noticed that as the ice melted and the beverage warmed, the slush started tasting more and more artificial. Like the cheap fruit punch they serve at kid's birthday parties. But this smells funny, like something has been added to it."

Briggs rubbed his chin as he stared down at Mr. Samuels. "Interesting. Would you mind terribly taking a whiff of his mouth to see if you can find the same scent?"

"Not at all." I walked around to the side of the desk he was standing on. "That's what my sniffer is for, right?"

He glanced back toward the door to make sure no one was near. "For that and for the occasional kiss." He lightly kissed my nose. "Seems our movie night turned out a little differently than planned."

"I don't know about that." I brazenly looked him up and down. "I think I like this Maltese Falcon style Bogart even better than the Casablanca one."

A clamor in the narrow corridor signaled that the coroner had arrived. I stooped down and lowered my nose near Mr. Samuels' mouth. I pulled back instinctively and fanned my face.

"Did you smell something?" Briggs asked.

"Yes, I think he had garlic for lunch. It's strong." I leaned forward once more and twitched my nose side to side, hoping to separate out the various smells. When I worked as a perfumer, I trained myself to isolate each fragrance. It wasn't easy, but with a bit of concentration, I could turn off certain odors to pinpoint the ones I was looking for. It was a skill that made me highly sought after in the perfume industry.

"Detective Briggs, how are you? I'm Doctor Hershonhaus, but you can call me Doc Patty. I'm Nate's assistant." The woman's voice behind me was unfamiliar. Normally, Nate Blankenship showed up when there was a dead body. Apparently, he'd taken on an assistant.

I finished my nasal inspection and managed to catch a faint trace of the same odd smell I found in the cup.

I pushed to my feet. The coroner, Dr. Patty, was less than five feet tall and with glasses so thick it seemed her eyes took up half her face. She shuffled forward on her sensible flat shoes. Her magnified eyes stared down at the body on the floor.

"Certainly wasn't a heart attack," she said confidently. I'd observed Nate Blankenship examine a body several times, but I'd never seen him jump straight to a conclusion without first surveying the victim. Even when the cause of death was obvious like a gun shot.

"Because his tie is still tight around his neck?" Briggs asked, jumping back to his earlier theory.

Doc Patty's enormously magnified eyes swept down again. "That is occasionally a clue, but his skin pallor is all wrong. Heart attack victims usually have a mottled, almost flushed cast to their skin. Especially if death occurred recently. She popped her face back up. "Do we have any estimate on the time of death yet?"

I spoke up. "I saw him alive and well just an hour ago. I was out at the concession stand as he was called into the projector room to solve a problem."

Doc Patty blinked at me. It was hard not to stare back at her with her thick lenses and gigantic gray-blue eyes. The glasses must have been too heavy for her nose because she kept pushing them up. "Oh yes, you must be the woman with hyperosmia who occasionally helps out with the cases." She looked at Briggs. "Nate mentioned you had an assistant." Her brows scrunched together lifting her heavy glasses high on her nose. "How did you happen to be here to see the victim alive?"

Briggs cleared his throat. "Doctor Hershon—Hersun—" He cleared it again. "Doctor Patty, if you could please examine the victim to find a cause of death, if one can be seen before the autopsy. I need to go make a call to his son." He turned back to me. "Miss Pinkerton, would you mind checking on the employees. I'm sure they are feeling anxious about tonight's tragic event."

"Yes, of course." I followed him down the hallway.

He flashed me an amused grin about the new coroner. "Nate mentioned he hired an assistant. Let's see what she finds." We walked into the lobby. Sally hurried across the room with a yellow sticky note. "Here is the phone number. His name is Dylan. As far as I know that is his only family besides his ex-wife."

"Thank you. Is there some place private I can make the call?"

Sally waved her hands around. "Every theater is vacant. Choose any place you like." Earlier, she was distressed and on the verge of sobs, but she seemed to have cooled her emotions. She spoke calmly as if the entire thing was already far in the past.

Briggs walked off with the phone number. I noticed Trinity sitting alone behind the concession stand sipping a cola. I walked over to see how she was faring.

"How are you doing, Trinity?"

She put her soda down and shrugged. "I don't know. I feel like I should be really sad. I mean he's dead, right?"

"Yes, yes he is."

"That's so weird. One minute he's storming about, throwing out orders, bossing people around and the next he's dead. Doesn't makes sense. Although, my mom told me her great granddad just fell over dead one day. He was getting up to put a log on the fire and he just kept going, face first into the hearth. They said he was gone before he hit the ground." She crinkled her nose. "Probably a good thing cuz falling face first has got to hurt."

"Never thought of that but you're right. And that does occasionally happen with a heart attack or stroke."

She picked up her soda, crunched the ice around with the straw and took a sip. Our brief chat had lightened her mood. It seemed like a good opportunity to find out what was happening right before Mr. Samuels' body was discovered.

"Trinity, when was the last time you saw Mr. Samuels alive?"

She chewed on the tip of her straw in thought, then let it go. "I remember now. He'd gone to the projector room. Then I didn't see him for awhile. I think he was checking time cards or something. He's really nitpicky about us clocking in and out on time." A tiny frown fell on her lips. "I guess I shouldn't talk mean about him. It's just hard to find nice things to say. Except, he did once wear a pair of socks around Halloween that had skeletons on them. It was so not like him. They were cool. I think they glowed in the dark."

"See, there's always something nice to say about everyone. But did you see him at all after that?"

"Yeah, he stopped behind the counter to get a cup of ice water. He was acting kind of strange." She lowered her voice. "I know this sounds weird but he was moving kind of unsteady, you know, swaying back and forth like maybe he'd been drinking. First time I'd ever seen him act like that. He filled his cup and sort of stumbled against the counter. I asked if he was all right, but he didn't answer me." Trinity's eyes grew wet with tears. "This is my fault. I should have told someone. He wasn't feeling well, and I didn't say anything."

I took her hand. "No. You asked. He just didn't answer. Don't blame yourself."

My words seemed to calm her worries. "So . . . you and the

handsome Detective Briggs?" she asked in a lightning fast topic switch.

I smiled. "I'm sure Detective Briggs will want to talk to everyone before you go home for the night. It should be soon. Make sure you tell him everything you just told me."

CHAPTER 13

*D*oc Patty was definitely more theatrical than Nate Blankenship. She instructed her two person crew to take various photos of the body while she stood back making every expression from deep, thoughtful concentration to quiet alarm. In the end, she had several conclusions spanning from a brain aneurysm to possible poisoning. I sensed some frustration from Briggs when she announced loudly that he might very well have been murdered. It was something Briggs liked to keep quiet whenever any of the victim's acquaintances were still within earshot.

Since the theater was located in the town of Mayfield, four city police officers were sent to the scene to take statements and collect evidence while Doc Patty and her team prepared Mr. Samuels for transportation to the morgue.

Briggs was writing down a few notes while the activity swirled around him. He was still recovering from having to inform Samuels' son about the death.

"I like this casual detective attire," I noted as I peered over his shoulder at his notes.

"You and me both. I wish the higher ups would relax the detective dress code, but it's still suit and tie. During a heat wave, a suit is nothing short of torture."

"If it makes you feel any better, the first time I saw you in your detective's suit and tie, I thought you looked handsome enough to be a television detective."

A line creased the side of his mouth. "If only I got the same pay as those television detectives." He closed his notebook. "Since Doc Patty has already announced to the world that this is a murder investigation, I thought I might go out back to the alley and the trash bins to see if I can find any evidence. Dylan Samuels should be here in about fifteen minutes. I want to be back inside when he arrives. He sounded extremely upset. I'm sure he'll have a hundred questions. For which, I won't have any answers."

"I'll join you for some sniffing. Whatever was in that drink had a weird sweet smell. Did Trinity tell you about Mr. Samuels acting strangely just before he died?"

I followed him through hallway to the emergency exit.

"She said he was stumbling as if he'd been drinking." He opened the door and held it for me. "There was no evidence of alcohol in his office. Did you smell any on his mouth?"

"No. I think we can rule out that he was drinking."

A large trash bin was pressed up against the outside wall of the theater. "Of course, we'll have to wait for Doc Patty's report," he said the name with a touch of mockery. "But I agree. Unsteadiness and stumbling around could have been the early symptoms of poisoning."

Not to be overwhelmed by smells, I stood back while he lifted the heavy rubber lid. Once some of the odors trapped inside the hot can had been released, I stepped forward.

Briggs peered inside. "Interesting." He gave the lid a toss. It fell back and away from the bin giving us a better view of the contents. I held my breath and cautiously approached the lip of the bin. Since it contained trash from the movie theater and not leftovers from a diner or restaurant, the odor hovering over it was manageable for my sensitive nose.

I peered inside, and my gaze followed Briggs' line of sight. An extraordinary amount of rat poison boxes were piled in one corner. The seemingly empty containers of peanut butter flavored rat bait were sitting on top of the other debris, which included things one would expect to find in a theater's trash bin. Crushed paper products, disposed drink cups, popcorn buckets, napkins and empty candy boxes filled the container halfway to the top. Some of the waste was wrapped in removable trash bags and tied neatly at the top to keep things sealed up.

"Seems like the theater had a rat problem," I noted.

"Yes but that's not the interesting part." Briggs pointed into the bin. "Look how the boxes are all piled in one corner, almost as if someone took the time to stack them neatly. The rest of the debris has just been tossed into the bin without thought. Like one would expect."

"Hmm, you're right. It is sort of odd. And frankly, if my business had been infested by rats, I think I might hide the evidence by shoving the boxes into one of the opaque trash bags."

"Good point." Briggs walked around the side of the can to the corner where the rat poison boxes were stacked. He pulled one free from the stack and checked out the label. "According to the graphics, the poison comes in pellet form. The box is only the outer packaging. The pellets are sealed in a bag to keep them fresh," he read off the box. "So where are the bags?"

"Maybe Samuels has the rat poison stored inside somewhere in the bags. Maybe he decided to get rid of the boxes so no one saw that he had a rat problem." I looked wide-eyed at James. "Maybe he accidently ate some pellets thinking they were—I don't know—candy?" I laughed. "Scratch that idea. I'm sounding silly. Must be the trash odor getting to me."

Briggs walked around with the box. "I know there are a lot of odors around us, and the box is empty but would you mind?" He held it up for me to smell.

I took several long whiffs. "I do smell something similar to peanut butter. Mostly the box just smells like cardboard and a crazy carnival mix of popcorn, soda and candy all glued together with that one-of-a-kind trash can fragrance. Whatever I smell, it's not even close to the scent in the lemon-lime cup."

Briggs put the box back into the bin and glanced inside from the new angle. His eyes swept across the pile of garbage, then his face snapped back toward the front of the bin. "Hold on." He circled back to the front of the trash can. I hopped up on tiptoes and looked inside to see what had caught his interest. A white plastic bottle of coolant was sitting between two stuffed garbage bags.

"Coolant is poisonous, right?" I asked.

"It sure is. It's considered extra dangerous because it has a sweet taste. Most adults would know not to guzzle it, but it's not something you leave around for kids and pets. And it comes in bright colors." He pulled on the plastic glove he'd had the fore-thought to carry with him for a garbage can tour. He hoisted himself up and leaned over the edge of the can to pluck the coolant bottle free. There was no lid. He shook it to show me it was empty. "Looks like someone used all of it. The question is—did they use it only for automotive purposes or for something more sinister?" He took a whiff and rubbed his nose with the back of his hand. "It smells faintly fruity to me, but I think we need the expert to give it a whiff."

Briggs held the bottle for me to smell. I lowered my nose and breathed in. I did it twice just to make sure.

"Yep." I looked up at Briggs. "That's what I smelled in Mr. Samuels' slush cup."

Briggs looked at the bottle in his hand. "Looks like we have murder by lemon-lime poison."

CHAPTER 14

B riggs gave the bottle to the Mayfield officers to mark as evidence. Sally saw us standing out front near the squad cars and came out to fetch Briggs. She was an entirely different person than a few hours ago. She was wringing her hands and playing nonstop with the bracelets on her wrists. I thought back to what Shauna had mentioned about Sally being in her anxiety support group. She was definitely on a thinner thread than earlier.

"Detective Briggs," she said quickly, "Dylan Samuels is here, and he is very distraught. I looked around but couldn't find you." She once again moved the bracelets on her wrist, pushing them back farther only to have them slip forward to her hand again.

"Miss Pinkerton and I were collecting evidence." He seemed to sense he'd said just the wrong thing, but it was too late.

"Evidence?" Sally took a few short breaths and waved her hand in front of her face, causing her bracelets to jangle. "So the coroner was right? It was murder." Her face paled visibly as she said the word. "That's just horrible. Can you please go inside and talk to Dylan. I need to stay out here and catch my breath. I'm feeling slightly sick from all of this."

"Can I get you anything?" I asked. "A paper bag for breathing or a glass of water?"

She rubbed her forehead. "No, I just need fresh air."

Briggs and I started to walk away. He stopped and turned back to her. "One quick question, Ms. Applegate. Was the theater having a problem with rats?"

Her face blanched more. "Did you say rats?"

"Yes. Was there an infestation or something?" Briggs asked.

A weak, nervous laugh fell from her lips. "Gosh, I hope not. I'm scared to death of rats. If there was a problem, Mr. Samuels never mentioned it."

Briggs pulled out his notebook. "Thank you."

We found Dylan Samuels pacing the front of the concession stand, looking upset, which was no surprise given the circumstances. He spotted Detective Briggs and lumbered toward us. His face was red and his eyes puffy, indicating that he'd been crying.

"I haven't told my mother yet," Dylan said weakly as he approached us. "I need to talk to her in person. I had just reached the hospital when you phoned. I hadn't gone up to see her yet. I turned right back around and headed back to the theater." He wiped his palm over his thick, wavy hair before rubbing his hands together. "I don't understand. I was just here talking to him a few hours ago. It doesn't make sense. The coroner doesn't think it was a heart attack." He paced around some, which seemed to help ease the stress. He combed his hair with his fingers again and then stopped abruptly in front of Briggs. "If not a heart attack, then what? My father always ran on high octane gas, if you know what I mean. He was always uptight and he got upset easily." Briggs had fallen into his listening mode. He was highly skilled at just letting people talk. I knew he was cataloguing every word and mannerism and reaction. After all, family members were some of the first suspects in a murder investigation. Although, this particular victim did seem to have a lot of enemies or, at the very least, people who didn't like him.

Briggs pointed to one of the Casablanca prop tables to silently suggest they sit but Dylan shook his head. "I'm better standing at the moment," he insisted. "I'm very agitated. It's been a difficult few days. My mother just came out of open heart surgery."

"How is your mother?" I asked quietly. Dylan didn't seem to notice or mind my presence. My question took his mind off his father for a moment.

"She's doing well. They'll probably move her from intensive care tomorrow. My parents are divorced, but I know she wanted to see my dad before she went into surgery. He's always too busy." He covered his mouth and paused as he closed his eyes. "I'm sorry. I'm still talking about him in present tense." He sobbed once and swallowed deeply. "I have to get strong so I can tell my mom."

"Maybe it would be better if you gave her a few more days to recover before you break the news," Briggs suggested.

"I can't risk her hearing it from someone else. My dad's death was pretty public considering it happened in his theater in the middle of vintage movie night."

"Of course," Briggs said. "You're right."

Dylan's face turned angry. "What happened? I need to know as soon as possible. The coroner mentioned possible poisoning."

Briggs' cheek twitched with irritation. I predicted that he might have a talk with Doc Patty at some point during the night. "We won't know anything for certain until we have the autopsy report. Mr. Samuels, is there anyone you can think of who might have been angry enough at your dad to hurt him?" I was sure he knew the answer to the question, but he wanted to hear it from Dylan. And hear it he did.

Dylan crossed his arms tightly as if trying to contain himself.

"That horrid woman, Connie Wilkerson, the owner of the Starlight Theater. She has plenty of reason. My dad's theater gets most of the movie business in town. Connie has always been jealous of it. After that rundown theater of hers caught fire, she started a rumor that my dad paid someone to start it as a form of sabotage. His theater was already doing better than hers. Why on earth would he need to sabotage the Starlight?" He uncrossed his arms, and his thick shoulders relaxed. It seemed the release of rage was helping him cope with the stress of the night. "You need to pull her in for interrogation," he said sharply. "Right away."

"Yes, thank you. I'll be talking to Ms. Wilkerson soon," Briggs said calmly. "Mr. Samuels, you came to the theater tonight to see your father. I saw you when I was at the concession stand ordering popcorn for the movie."

His forehead rolled up. "You were here in the theater when the mur—" He covered his mouth and took a breath. "When my father died?"

"Yes. We came to watch Casablanca," Briggs explained. "What did you come to talk to your dad about?"

He shuffled his large feet beneath him again and shook his head. "I just wanted to let him know the surgery went well and that she wanted to see him soon. He got called off to fix a problem with the projector, so we didn't get a chance to finish our talk." He sobbed once. "That's the last time I saw him alive."

Briggs placed his hand on Dylan's arm. "We won't need anything else from you tonight. The coroner's office will get in contact with you tomorrow. Take care when driving to the hospital to see your mom. She'll need you to be well and strong during this time."

Dylan pulled a tissue out of his pocket and wiped his eyes. "Yes, you're right. Please let me know as soon as you've heard anything."

"I will. Good night, Mr. Samuels, and I truly am sorry."

We watched him walk toward the exit.

"He was extremely distraught," I said.

Briggs was still watching him. I could see the little detective gears spinning in his head, analyzing the last few minutes. Dylan's reaction seemed natural and entirely expected to me, but it seemed my *partner* had different thoughts.

CHAPTER 15

*B*riggs and I filled some cups with ice water to rehydrate. Sally had begun the process of shutting everything down for the night. She turned off the air conditioning first. It took only minutes before the outside heat seeped in to replace the cool air. The coroner had taken Mr. Samuels away, and the weary and bewildered employees looked ready to go home and leave the terrible night behind. I was certain the prospect of being jobless weighed heavy on their thoughts as well.

"I need to let these people go home," Briggs said. "We can head out soon too." His brown eyes looked extra warm under the overhead lights of the concession stand. "Sorry this movie night took such a turn south."

I reached for his hand. "Are you kidding? A murder mystery is always more fun than an old movie. Even one with Bogie." I cleared my throat. "Maybe fun was a tasteless word. After all, a man is dead. Let's just say intriguing. Especially when I'm with my favorite detective."

"And especially for me when I'm with my favorite nose."

I opened my mouth to protest, but he was already one step ahead.

"And the cute, smart assistant that comes with the nose, of course," he added . . . wisely.

I took a drink of ice water. "Nice save, Detective Briggs."

"Thank you, Miss Pinkerton." He drained his cup. "I think we have the source of poison with that empty bottle of coolant, but I'm going to ask the employees to open their lockers for a quick search before I dismiss everyone for the night. I'll have to make it voluntary for now. Sometimes a refusal speaks volumes. I think Miss Applegate is shutting down each theater. I'll go find her and tell her my plan."

Trinity came out of the restroom just then.

"I could get the first one done right now." Briggs nodded Trinity's direction, indicating he wanted me to ask her about the locker since I'd already formed a bond with her.

"Trinity." I walked over to meet her. "Detective Briggs is going to do a quick locker search. Voluntary, of course. Do you mind opening your locker?"

I expected an easy-going shrug. Instead, she bit her lip. Her eyes darted over to Briggs and back to me. "I—I don't have much in there. Just some sneakers and a sweatshirt. The theater lobby gets cold at night. Not tonight of course." She wiped a few tiny beads of sweat from her forehead. "Why is it so hot in here?"

"Sally is shutting down the theater for the night."

"Does that mean we'll be open tomorrow? We're all wondering if we still have jobs." Her eyes turned glassy. "It's too late in the summer to find another job. All the good ones are taken."

"I'm sure a decision will be made soon. In the meantime, you need to go home and rest. It's been a long, difficult night. Do you think Detective Briggs could glance inside your locker?"

She nodded weakly. "Sure. I guess. I mean, like I said, there isn't much inside of it."

We followed Trinity to the employee lounge. A set of ten green lockers stood next to the time clock. Two round plastic tables with plastic chairs sat in the center of the small, windowless room. An ancient looking microwave sat on the counter next to a coffee pot. Someone had stuck a piece of paper on the front of the microwave that read 'use at your own risk'.

Trinity led us to the second locker from the end. It seemed she'd just realized she was the only person opening a locker. She looked back at us. "Will anyone else have to open their locker?"

Briggs smiled. "Yes, I'll ask everyone. And remember, I'm not the school principal. I'm just looking for something that might help us figure out how Mr. Samuels died."

"All right." She pulled a small key out from her uniform pocket and unlocked the door. She opened it and stepped aside. As Trinity moved out of the way, I noticed her face drop. She stared down at the ground, avoiding eye contact.

Briggs opened the door wider. A photo of Trinity and Justin standing at a party holding hands was taped to the inside of the door. A sweatshirt had been crumpled into a ball and thrown on top of a pair of worn out sneakers. The only things out of place were two containers of salt.

Trinity snuck a peek toward the locker as Briggs reached in and took out the containers. He shook them. They were empty.

"I like to eat salt on my popcorn, but Mr. Samuels doesn't let us use much. He says it's too expensive."

"Salt?" I asked. "Salt is one of the cheapest things at the grocery store."

Trinity's cheeks were a few shades deeper. She fidgeted with the brass buttons on her uniform. "I told you, Mr. Samuels was really cheap."

"So your boss is too miserly to buy salt, and you have a rather unhealthy salt habit," Briggs said wryly. He shook the empty cardboard canisters once more to emphasize his point. "Or just maybe you were behind the salt sabotage on the soda machine."

Trinity covered her face and crumpled into sobs. "I did it. I did it."

I shot a wide-eyed look at Briggs. Was it possible the sweet, fun Trinity had poisoned her own boss? He was unkind and possibly even despicable but murder?

It seemed Briggs understood the confession differently. "So you put salt in the machine?"

Trinity dropped her hands. Her face was splotchy and pink. "Yes, I poured salt into the machine. I was so mad at Mr. Samuels, I couldn't stop myself. Yesterday, a bunch of Justin's friends showed up for a movie. Mr. Samuels yelled at Justin right in front of all of them about some stupid thing like leaving the trash can lid open. Justin was so embarrassed. I decided Mr. Samuels needed to be embarrassed too, so I poured salt in the machine."

Briggs kept the salt containers but closed the locker. "Do you have any acquaintance with Connie Wilkerson?"

Trinity looked baffled. "Who?"

"She owns the Starlight Movie Theater at the other end of the street," Briggs explained.

"Oh right. No, I don't know her other than I know Mr. Samuels didn't like her. He thought she was trying to ruin his business." She covered her mouth. "Oh my gosh, I just figured out why you asked me that." Her face turned red. "She had nothing to do with the salt plan. That was all me. Justin was so mad about being chewed out in front of his friends, we didn't even hang out last night. We were supposed to get ice cream and play video games but he was too upset." She moved closer. "I do think that lady from the Starlight might have done something to Mr. Samuels. From what I've heard, she still thinks Mr. Samuels caused the fire at the Starlight. And who knows? Mr. Samuels was a mean guy." Her hands flew to her mouth again. "I'm sorry. I shouldn't talk badly about the dead. My mom told me that after my Great Aunt Ursula died. She was ninety-eight, so I didn't think it was such a big deal. She was such a sour puss. She never liked us kids. She used to give us each a set of towels for Christmas. Who gives kids towels? I guess she thought we all needed to take more baths."

I held back a smile as Briggs attempted to bring Trinity back to the topic.

"Yes, I had an uncle who gave us coupons for a hair cut at his barber shop," Briggs added. "Now back to Ms. Wilkerson, have you ever seen her here at the Mayfield Four?"

"Hmm, let me think." Trinity tapped her pink fingernail against her chin. She seemed to have gotten past the small guilt trip over sabotaging the soda machine, and she was back to her bubbly self. "Wait, there was that time during winter break when she came here to see him. She rushed right past the ticket window and into the theater and straight into his office. They yelled at each other for a few minutes. Mr. Samuels threatened to call the police on her for coming inside without a ticket. His face was so red, I thought he was going to have a heart—" Again her hands covered her mouth. "Sorry again. Guess it's been a long night."

"Yes it has," I agreed.

Briggs was jotting down a few notes. "Do you know what they fought about?"

"Yes I do," she said, seemingly excited she was having her words written down in a detective's notebook. "The Starlight was serving hot chocolate in the theater for the holidays. There was a big peppermint colored banner hanging below the marquee inviting everyone in for a good movie and a cup of hot chocolate. Mr. Samuels noticed the hot chocolate was popular, so he copied her. He put up a big banner too, only his had snowflakes. She came to yell at him about stealing her idea. Can't blame her. But Mr. Samuels was always arguing with people. The popcorn vendor, the carpet cleaner, the paper towel company, you name it. Even tonight, his son was only here for a few minutes, but I could hear them arguing."

That last detail caught both of our attentions. Briggs looked up from his notebook. "Mr. Samuels was arguing with his son tonight? Could you hear what they were fighting about?"

She shook her head. "I could only hear loud voices behind the wall. I don't know what they were talking about. Since Mr. Samuels was always yelling, I hardly paid attention to it."

Briggs closed his notebook. "Thank you, Miss Falco. You can go home. Do you have a ride?"

"Yes. My mom is on her way."

Briggs and I walked out to find the other employees.

"Interesting," I said. "Dylan Samuels didn't mention any argument with his dad."

Briggs put his notebook into his pocket. "Yes. I find that interesting too."

CHAPTER 16

*J*ustin had wasted no time removing the red double-breasted usher's coat and matching hat once it was confirmed Mr. Samuels was dead. He had balled the coat up and thrown it in his locker. He pulled it out, along with the hat, to show Briggs that the only other things he had inside his locker were the t-shirt, shorts and sneakers he'd worn into work.

"Thanks for showing us the locker," Briggs said. "I know you've already given your statement, but do you remember where you were between the time the projector was fixed and when you came in to ask for my help?"

"Yeah, like I told the officer, I saw Mr. Samuels head up to the projector room. I took my fifteen minute break right after that. When I came back inside, I looked for Sally to see if there was anything else she needed me to do. I couldn't find her, so I went straight to the maintenance closet to get the things I needed to clean theater one. The movie was close to finished. It's my job to clean up trash in between shows."

Briggs looked up. "Since you are part of the custodial team, do you know if the theater was having any problems with rats?"

The question caused him to laugh. "You mean like the kind with tails, or tattle tales, cuz we've got a few of those around here too."

Briggs was amused but he kept his cool. "I mean the kind with tails."

Justin looked at me almost as if to see if Briggs was serious. "I've never seen one in the theater. But I wouldn't put it past Connie Wilkerson from over at the Starlight to buy some at the pet store and plant them in the theater. She hates Samuels." He paused and rubbed his nose. "I mean hated. Kinda weird having to talk about him in past tense all of a sudden. Heck, he was just chewing me out a few hours ago and now he's dead." He seemed to want to walk back the last sentence. "Not that I'd off him or anything like that. He was a terrible guy to work for but I'm more into chillin' and riding waves. I take life one day at a time."

"Yes, I can see that," Briggs said. "Do you know anyone working here who might not be quite as *chill* as you? Someone who disliked Mr. Samuels?"

"Nah, not here. But I think Samuels did set that fire at the Starlight. Maybe Connie wanted to get revenge. Yesterday, someone poured salt into the soda machine. People were spitting cherry cola and orange soda everywhere. It was gross. I think Connie might have paid someone to dump salt in it when no one was looking."

Briggs shifted a glance my direction. Apparently, Trinity had decided to secretly avenge Justin's honor.

The topic of the salty soda machine spurred the same question into my head as the one that Briggs asked. "I understand that Mr. Samuels yelled at you in front of all your friends. I had my dad do that to me once, and I was mad as heck about it. How did that make you feel?"

The new topic made Mr. Chill a little less chill. His otherwise slack posture (to go with the chillin' part) grew rigid. Red flush crept up his neck to mingle with his suntanned skin. "Didn't make me happy. But that doesn't mean I killed the guy." His posture relaxed again. "Can I go now?" He reached into his locker and rummaged through his clothes to get to the sneakers. The t-shirt piled on top rolled out.

I stooped down and picked it up. A scent grabbed my attention. I discretely took a whiff of the shirt and handed it to him.

Briggs put away his notebook. "You can head home. Do you have a ride?"

He scoffed and looked more than a little insulted. "I've got my own car." He slammed shut the locker.

"Of course," Briggs said and backed out of the way. "Drive safely."

Justin sauntered out of the employee lounge.

"We should probably follow him to his car," I suggested.

"He's a big kid." He suddenly sensed I had more to go with my suggestion. Sometimes we were riding along each other's wave lengths. Tonight was one of those nights. "Why?"

"Because the t-shirt he dropped smelled like coolant."

CHAPTER 17

*M*y stunning revelation that Justin's shirt smelled like coolant sent Briggs and I out to the parking lot. Justin was sitting in an old truck trying to turn the engine over but not having a great deal of luck.

He was surprised to see us standing outside his truck and rolled down the window. "Do you still need to talk to me?" His voice was edged with irritation, which might have had more to do with the stubborn truck motor than us.

"Yes, if you could just step out of the truck for a second, I'd like to ask you a couple of questions," Briggs said it calmly, but Justin still looked alarmed by the request.

The door creaked as Justin pushed it open. "I told you, I didn't do anything. I was just doing my job tonight."

Briggs pulled out his notebook and opened to the page he'd started for Justin. "Mr. Lakeford, I just have a few more questions. I'm absolutely not accusing you of anything. You mentioned you went on a break during the time in question. Did you talk to anyone or hang out with anyone on that break?"

Justin raked his thick hair back with his fingers. His wavy locks had that sun and salt bleached look as if he spent a lot of time sitting out in the water on his board. He was just a kid. He certainly didn't seem like the murdering type but then I'd been surprised before.

"Mr. Samuels always made the break schedule so that none of us could hang out together." He added an eye roll. "He said we'd stay too long on our breaks if we were talking and laughing with our buddies. He didn't want us to enjoy one second of working for him," he added with a huff. "I came out here, sat in my car and looked at my phone. We're only allowed to use phones for emergencies when we're in the theater."

While Briggs talked to Justin, I circled around the front of the car. I could smell some of the usual odors that came from a car, especially an older less digitized model, burning oil, the acrid scent of various motor lubricants and something that smelled distinctly like coolant.

Briggs knew exactly what I was doing. He peered my way for a second. I nodded to let him know the car had recently been filled with coolant.

"Mr. Lakeford, have you recently used a coolant product on your car?" Briggs asked.

The question made Justin's brows raise right into his pile of wavy hair. "Y-Yeah," he said with confusion. "I need a new radiator but couldn't afford one because Samuels was so cheap." He wasn't holding back on his unabashed dislike for his late boss. "I keep adding coolant, but this heat wave is making it worse. Is there a crime in trying to keep your car running?" His attitude was starting to grate on Briggs' nerves. His jaw tightened just enough for me to notice.

"Certainly no crime in keeping your car running," Briggs said just sharply enough to let Justin know to cool it. "Where is the bottle of coolant? Do you still have it?"

Justin's defensive posture softened after Briggs' discrete admonition. "I left it here by the car. I bought it on the way to work and filled my radiator when I got here. But I couldn't get the stupid cap off, so I had to break the lid. I was planning to walk back to the trash bin and toss it after work. It's gone now, so someone must have taken it."

Briggs wrote down the statement. Listening in on the conversation, nothing about his coolant story sounded forced or made up. Briggs closed his notebook. "Thanks. You've been helpful." He looked at the truck. "Do you need some help getting it started?"

Justin's earlier attitude had smoothed out. He looked tired and ready to get home. "Nah, it just takes a few tries to start. Can I go?"

"Yes, drive safely."

CHAPTER 18

*B*riggs sighed audibly as we walked back into the theater. "Considering this was my night off, I'm tired."

I gave his arm an apologetic squeeze. "This was my fault. I came up with the Casablanca plan. I had no idea the night would end up like this."

"That makes two of us."

Sally was the last person left in the theater. Her face was drawn and tired as she wiped down the soda machine.

"Is there anything we can do to help you close up?" I asked.

My voice startled her. She turned around. "I thought you two had gone. I'm almost finished. I left a message for Dylan Samuels. I don't know what to do with tonight's cash. Mr. Samuels was the only person with the code to the safe. Did you get everything you needed with the statements and locker checks?"

Briggs smiled politely. "Yes, but I have one more locker to check if you don't mind."

It took her a second to understand what he was asking. Her lack of clarity was understandable. The trauma of the night and having to shut down the theater on her own was starting to show in gray circles beneath her eyes.

"Oh yes, of course. My locker is mostly empty. I rarely use it. The kids like to bring comfortable shoes and clothes to change into, but I don't wear one of those heavy, uncomfortable red uniforms. I don't bring spare clothes." We followed her to the employee lounge as she spoke.

Her phone beeped just as we reached the lockers. She opened the door, revealing nothing more than one bottle of aspirin and a banana that was a few days past ripe. After some of the stories I'd heard about Mr. Samuels, a bottle of aspirin seemed entirely appropriate.

She glanced at the text on her phone and groaned in disappointment. "Looks as if I'll have to stick around for awhile. Dylan is coming back to the theater to take care of the cash. He doesn't have a key."

That statement caught our attention. "Dylan Samuels doesn't have keys to his father's theater?" Briggs asked. "Seems like it would be a good security measure to have someone he could trust keep a spare key."

"As far as I know, I'm the only one with a spare key. Last winter, before Christmas, I had the flu. I was sick in bed with a fever and terrible aches and pains. Mr. Samuels got delayed at home, so he called me to open up the theater. I live just a few miles away. When I asked him if his son could open up because I was terribly sick and it was freezing outside, he said Dylan didn't have a key." She twisted her mouth into a frown. "He also told me if I didn't open up, I'd be fired."

I couldn't hide my disgust, even though I knew Briggs wouldn't like it. "The man was truly without conscience."

"It seems there were a lot of things not to like about that man," Briggs responded. It wasn't like him to voice his opinion out loud, at least not to people he was interviewing, but Mr. Samuels was a special case. The miserly, mean stories about him just kept piling up. "Ms. Applegate, I know you made a statement to the officers earlier but would you mind filling me on a few details. Where were you during the time between the start of the Casablanca film and the moment Justin told you Mr. Samuels was on the floor of his office?"

The question threw her slightly. She began fidgeting with her bracelets, something I'd seen her do often during the last few hours. "I was tending to an issue in the men's bathroom." The statement produced a touch of pink in her cheeks. "One of the toilets keeps getting clogged."

"Yes, I saw the closed sign on the bathroom when I went to use the ladies' room," I added.

Briggs wrote down a few notes before continuing. "It's a little out of your job description, isn't it? Plumbing in the men's room?"

A nervous, dry laugh shot from her mouth. "Yes, there were a lot of things Mr. Samuels required me to do that were out of my job description. He was too cheap to hire a plumber, so he asked me to deal with it. I unwittingly let it be known that my dad was a plumber and that I'd apprenticed for him after high school. At least until I realized I didn't have the stomach for clogged plumbing or climbing beneath houses. I was working on the—" She cleared her throat. "The restroom issue for a good thirty minutes. Then, as you might expect, I walked outside for a few minutes of fresh air. When I came back inside, Justin was racing toward me as if he'd seen a ghost. That's when he told me Mr. Samuels was on the floor of his office not moving. I checked on him and immediately called the ambulance."

Briggs finished writing the statement.

Sally relaxed some, seemingly relieved to have her part of the story finished. "You know, we all complain about working here, but the reality is going to hit us tomorrow when it seems we are jobless. It's hard to know what will happen to the theater. I don't think Dylan has any interest in this business. He rarely spoke to his dad. He only came around a lot lately because of his mom's health problems. Not sure why," she said sadly. "It's not like his father gave him any support on that matter."

"Trinity told me you are responsible for the vintage movie night," I said. "The decorations were wonderful. It really felt like we'd stepped into Rick's gin joint. Sans the gin, of course. Maybe the Starlight Theater can use your talent. Or maybe if Dylan sells to another theater owner, he'll make sure to put in a good word for you."

Her cheeks blushed again. "To tell the truth, after the flu incident, I pleaded with Connie to take me on as assistant manager. I promised to help her turn the Starlight around. But she's been struggling so much since the fire, she can't afford to hire me." She drew in a deep breath. "Enough of my feeling sorry for myself. A man has died, after all. Even if there won't be a sea of tears at his funeral, it's a tragedy."

"Yes it is," Briggs said. "If you don't mind, we're going to wait out in the lobby for Dylan Samuels. I have just a few more questions for him."

"That's fine." She crossed her arms around herself. "I'm actually glad you're staying. After what happened tonight, this theater feels big, dark and a little sinister."

CHAPTER 19

*D*ylan Samuels walked into the mostly dark theater looking rightly somber. He was a big man with a broad shoulder span and a thick chest and belly that, for some reason, reminded me of a bull. Yet, he didn't look confident like a bull. Even with a large shoulder span, he looked crumpled as if someone had hit him in the gut. It seemed like a normal appearance considering that his dad was recently murdered and his mother was in intensive care in the hospital. I'm not entirely sure I would even be able to stand upright if I'd suffered the same.

Upon seeing him, Briggs seemed hesitant to approach him. He wanted to clarify Dylan's last talk with his dad. Trinity had mentioned that they had argued. That would certainly be something of note in a murder investigation.

I was quickly trying to come up with a reason to get closer to the man, just to check for the coolant scent, but short of walking up to hug him, I couldn't come up with a plausible excuse.

One thing was certain, he was more than surprised to see Briggs and I still standing in the theater.

"Detective Briggs, I didn't expect you to be here. Have you found out anything?"

"I haven't heard anything definite from the coroner yet. We stayed around because Sally was feeling a little uneasy alone in the theater."

"Well, I'm here now, so we don't need to keep you any longer. Please let me know the second you hear something." He seemed anxious for us to leave, or maybe he was just anxious to be done with the night himself.

"How is your mother?" Briggs asked. "I hope the news didn't set her recovery back."

Dylan walked behind the concession counter and helped himself to a bag of chocolate covered peanuts. "If you'll excuse me, the only food I've had tonight was popcorn." He ripped open the bag. "I didn't make it to the hospital. I called halfway there to check on her and they told me she was sleeping. I decided it was too soon to tell her. Then Sally called about the cash, so I turned around and headed back to the theater."

"Mr. Samuels, I know this has been a trying time for you, but I need to ask you something." Briggs hesitated. "An employee noted that they heard you and your father arguing, rather loudly. You didn't mention an argument when I talked to you earlier. Can I ask what you were fighting about?"

His face reddened and contorted. I couldn't tell if it was anger, indignation or sorrow that made his large face squish up almost as if it was made of dough. "Please, it's too painful to think about." He covered his mouth with the side of his fist. It took him a second to continue. "I didn't mention it because it's too painful to know that the last moments I spent with my dad were in a heated argument." He pulled a tissue from his pocket and wiped his eyes.

"I'll get you a cup of water," I said and rushed away. I'd found a reason to get close enough to the man to get a whiff of his clothes or, at the very least, his hand.

Dylan's large frame was more shriveled than when he walked inside. He looked close to passing out. Briggs helped him to one of the chairs in the center of the lobby. He sat with a thud and rested his head back with eyes closed.

I reached them with the cup of water.

"Here you go, Mr. Samuels." I leaned over, getting as close to him as possible without it seeming like an odd invasion of personal space. Rather than place the cup on the table, I waited for him to take hold of it. My plan worked. His fingers rubbed against mine as he took hold of the cup. There was no scent of coolant on his clothes.

I stepped back. Briggs pulled out the chair next to him and sat.

I turned away and discretely smelled my own hand. I smelled traces of parmesan. I'd nearly forgotten about seeing Dylan standing behind the concession stand showering a bucket of popcorn with parmesan cheese. His dad had told him then that he didn't have any more time to talk. That was just before Mr. Samuels rushed up to the projector room.

Dylan drained the cup of water.

Sally came out from the employee lounge. "Oh good, you're here. Detective Briggs and Miss Pinkerton were kind enough to wait with me. I have the money counted and placed in paper bands. I didn't want to use the office"—her voice trailed off, and she looked at me—"It didn't seem appropriate for me to sit at his desk." She caught a tiny sob. It seemed to be a genuine display of emotion and not just one put on for Dylan Samuels.

Briggs nodded. "We are almost through here, Ms. Applegate." It was his polite way of saying he needed for her to leave them alone.

She took the hint. "Of course. I'll just go back into the lounge and wait." She shuffled slowly off. Earlier in the evening, before the murder, she moved with the alacrity of an enthused cheerleader, excited to treat people to a night in Casablanca, but that spirit had drained away completely.

Briggs didn't waste any more time. It was getting close to midnight, and we were both tired. "Mr. Samuels," he started but didn't need to finish his question.

"We fought about my mother," Dylan snapped. The cup of water had apparently revived him. "I just wanted him to visit her. I didn't think it was too much to ask. They were married for twenty-five years, after all. It would have made her feel better to see him. But he couldn't be bothered." His voice went up a few octaves, but he kept a lid on his anger. "That's what we argued about. Don't you think I had a right to be mad? Wouldn't you be mad if it was your mother?" he asked Briggs.

"Yes, yes I would be." Briggs didn't take out his notebook. He patted Dylan on the shoulder. "We're going to see ourselves out. Try and get some rest. I'll let you know as soon as I hear something."

Dylan stood from the chair and nodded. "See that you do."

CHAPTER 20

*I*t seemed there was the slightest break in temperature as I walked from my car to the shop. It was still too early to know for sure, but it seemed the worst was over. Kingston seemed to notice too. He soared on ahead to stretch his wings. He circled right back like a boomerang though when his arch nemesis, a mockingbird who nested nearby, shot out of nowhere and chased angrily after him. Kingston landed on the roof of the shop, looking both frightened and humiliated. The mockingbird landed just a few feet away and stared at Kingston, her long tail lifting victoriously up and down like a lever. Of course there was nothing much I could do. The war between mockingbirds and crows was a longstanding tradition in the bird world. But like a worried mom, I hated to see his confidence shredded by a bully. Even a bully who was a quarter his size.

I stopped and stared up at my crow. "Come inside, King. Remember, you get to spend all day inside air conditioning nibbling on treats, and she's stuck out here in the sticky air searching for worms."

I opened the door and tucked myself aside, knowing full well that Kingston would swoop right past me, anxious to get away from the mockingbird. His wings fluttered against my shoulder as he soared past, landing with a clatter on his perch.

The shop phone rang the second I shut the door. I hurried over and picked it up. "Pink's Flowers."

"Hi, Lacey, this is Jazmin Falco. I've changed my mind about the first peony bouquet. I've decided the buttercups look too much like Easter brunch instead of a wedding. Can I come back by this morning and look at the bouquets again?" While I was relieved not to have to chase down out of season buttercups, something told me this wouldn't be her last change of mind.

"Yes, of course and we don't have to choose from my examples. I can show you a catalog. That will give you a broader range of choices." Even as I suggested it, I knew I was opening up a possibility for a long, teetering decision session. I normally offered a finite number of choices for no other reason except that it saved the client from having to agonize for hours over too many choices.

"That sounds perfect. I'm heading right over, if that's all right."

"Yes, of course." I waved to Ryder as he walked inside the shop. Kingston dropped right down off his perch and trotted quickly behind Ryder's long strides as he headed to the office to put away his lunch. My bird was feeling down about the embarrassing morning and obviously wanted an early treat to wash away the blues. He knew Ryder was an easy target.

"Great, we'll be there soon," Jazmin said and hung up. I wondered who was included in 'we'. Trinity had had a late, stressful night. I doubted she'd be up for another long flower decision session. Maybe the groom was coming this time. That was always a good thing. The grooms tended to get antsy quickly, and that usually prompted a faster decision.

I could actually hear the clicking of Kingston's talons on the floor as he continued trailing behind Ryder on his way to the shop front.

Ryder twisted around and checked behind him. "What does Kingston want?" he asked.

"What do you think?" I replied. "He had a bad morning. That wily, little mockingbird was harassing him. Now he's trying to make himself feel better with food." I paused after my statement. "My gosh, he really is turning human. Go ahead and give him a couple treats before I have to call a bird therapist."

Ryder plucked the treat can from its shelf. Kingston skittered behind him back to his perch. As he dropped the treats into the treat bowl, Ryder stretched up to gaze across the street to Lola's Antiques. He leaned side to side and stared that direction even after feeding Kingston.

"Are you looking for someone?" I asked. Lola was not expected back until next week. Her cousin had been lucky. The heat wave had kept customers to a minimum. The antique shop was so cluttered with items, it was always a little unwelcoming on a hot day.

Ryder pulled his attention from the front window. "Huh? Oh no. Not really. It's just that Shauna stopped me on my way out last night. She looked sort of pale and shaky. She claimed that the antique rocker in the back of the shop had been rocking back and forth on its own. I told her Late Bloomer probably knocked into it, but she seemed convinced an invisible spirit was trolling her inside the shop. I just wondered if she'd calmed herself yet. She looked pretty anxious."

"Uh oh, that's probably not good. Shauna told me she attends a support group for anxiety."

He shook his head. "Why would she have asked Shauna to watch the shop? That's just like Lola not to think about others when she flies off on her continental vacations."

I arched a brow to let him know, in case he didn't already, that he sounded petulant. He caught on fairly fast.

He raked his hair back with his fingers. "How is it that that woman always manages to bring out all my worst qualities," he muttered more to himself than in pursuit of advice.

But I was never great on keeping advice to myself. "*And* your best qualities," I said. "I think they call that a relationship."

"Right again, boss. You should switch your profession."

"Maybe I should." I laughed as I headed to the refrigerator to pull out the peony bouquets.

"Hey, weren't you at the Mayfield Four last night?" Ryder asked as I came around the corner with the flowers. "I heard the owner was killed right in his office."

I froze in my steps. "How did you hear that?"

"It was all over social media this morning. So it's true?"

I placed the bouquets on the island. "It's not certain yet that it was murder, but things are leaning that direction. We were an hour into Casablanca when one of the ushers came in to get James. Wasn't exactly a dream date but life around town is never boring."

"I'll say. Ghosts in rocking chairs and murdered theater owners. What's next?" Just as he said it, the bell on the door clanged loudly and Lola's cousin, Shauna, burst inside the shop. Her eyes were round with fear, and she was panting to catch her breath.

Ryder and I both rushed to her side. "I don't have a paper bag," I told her in as calm a tone as I could muster under the circumstances.

She shook her head, cupped her hands over her mouth and took a few deep, steadying breaths. We waited patiently for her to gather her wits. It seemed in one aspect, Ryder had been right. Shauna might not have been the best choice for running the antique shop.

When it seemed her breathing had slowed, Ryder took her arm and led her slowly to the stool. That was when I caught it. It was just the tiniest hint of admiration on Shauna's part, but I was sure I saw it. Even in the final stages of a panic attack, Shauna took a moment to favor Ryder with an eye twinkle.

She settled herself on the stool and smiled broadly at him. "Thank you," she said with an extra dose of sugar. "I didn't know what else to do, so I came here. I'm sure it's nothing, but I was sitting in the shop browsing through a couple magazines." She pulled her gaze from Ryder for a second to look at me. "There aren't many customers in this heat," she offered quickly, seemingly thinking she had to explain to me why she was just looking at magazines.

"Yes, we are slow too," I noted.

"Anyhow, I was looking at a magazine. Then I heard this strange howling sound." She closed her reddish-gold lashes and crooned a long ghostly sound. "Just like that. I swear it was coming from the storage room." She blinked her blue eyes at Ryder. "I hate to bother you, but do you think you could come across the street with me and check out the storage room?"

Ryder looked at me for permission.

"Of course," I said. "Ryder will take a look around. I'm sure there is a perfectly logical explanation for the sound you heard."

Shauna moved her head back and forth slowly. "I don't know about that. There wasn't anything logical about the sound I heard. It was just like this." Once again, she favored us with her unexplained howl impression.

Shauna was right in the middle of it when Jazmin walked inside the shop. Trinity shuffled in behind her on a pair of pink flip-flops. She looked energetic and bright eyed. Apparently, a shocking night of murder hadn't set her back too much.

Shauna saw there were customers and snapped her mouth shut. She didn't look too thrilled to see that two pretty young women had just entered the shop. She quickly led Ryder out the door and across the street to Lola's store.

"Good morning," I said. "I've pulled out the peony bouquets, including the one with buttercups, just in case you decide they are what you want after all. Although, I sort of agree with the Easter brunch look." I circled around to the open shelf side of the work island and pulled out my wedding bouquet notebook. It was filled with laminated photos of bridal bouquets. "Are you still set on peonies?" I circled back and set the notebook down in front of her.

"Yes. I promised my grandmother. She used them in her bouquets and my mom did too." She placed her large bag on the floor. Her tiny dog popped its head up and looked around before disappearing back into the purse.

I laughed. "Will your dog be in the ceremony? I've always pictured my wedding with Kingston." I motioned toward the perch. "I thought he could swoop in with the gold rings in his talons. I think he'd be quite the showstopper."

Trinity laughed.

Jazmin smiled. She didn't seem terribly entertained by my idea. "I think Tootsie would be terrified of all the people. But we are taking her on the honeymoon."

Trinity rolled her eyes. "She never goes anywhere without her precious, annoying little Tootsie." She made sure to put a strong accent on the double O in Tootsie.

"Just like I never seem to go anywhere without my annoying little sister." Jazmin sat on the stool and pulled the notebook closer. "And now that she doesn't have a job, she'll be bugging me even more."

Trinity placed her hands hard on her slim hips. "You don't know that. I still have a job. Someone has to keep the theater going. I think Sally will just be put in charge. That's even better than when Mr. Samuels was—" Her words trailed off as she seemed to conclude it wasn't nice to talk about a dead man.

"I'll give you some time to look," I said. "I've got a few bouquets to arrange. Just let me know if you have any questions."

Jazmin started to pore over the dozen or so pictures. Trinity was more interested in my bouquet arrangements than in her sister's wedding. She leaned against the work table at the back sink as I cut the stems on some pink roses.

"Where did that cute assistant guy go with that girl who was howling? And why was she howling?"

"Ryder was just going to help her with something. She's running the antique shop while Lola is out of town." I didn't feel like going into the whole story.

"She seemed kind of strange," she said snippily and then did an about face on topics. "Did you tell anyone about the salt? I'll lose my job if anyone finds out."

What I wanted to say was you should have thought of that before you poured salt into the machine. But I was part of the investigation, and it wasn't my place. "No one else knows." Since we were on the topic, I decided some unofficial prying wouldn't hurt. "Have you spoken to anyone? To your coworkers? Does anyone have a theory about who might have been wanting to harm Mr. Samuels?"

"I've only talked to Justin." She picked up one of the wilted roses I'd set aside and twirled it around in front of her nose for a whiff. "He says Detective Briggs thinks he killed Mr. Samuels."

I glanced up from my task. "Where did he get that idea?"

She shrugged casually, only I could tell the topic upset her. "He was asking Justin about the coolant he put in his car. Justin said that might have been the poison. He said the stuff looks and smells like green punch, so maybe someone snuck it inside the lemon-lime slush Mr. Samuels was drinking." She stared down. There was the slightest lip quiver happening beneath her freckled nose. "I gave him the drink, but I didn't put any poison in it," she said emphatically and loudly enough to catch her sister's attention.

Jazmin looked across the shop at us. "Is she bothering you, Lacey? Just send her back over here."

Trinity scoffed in the direction of her sister. "What am I? Your trained puppy? Not that your pup is anywhere near trained," she muttered as she turned back toward me.

I pushed a rose into the vase. "She's not bothering me," I called and then lowered my voice. "You don't need to worry about that. Detective Briggs will find the real killer." My statement didn't alarm her, which was a good thing. I hated to even consider her as a person of interest. She just didn't fit the mold of murderer. "That's why, if you hear anything from any of your coworkers, even Justin, you need to let me or Detective Briggs know right away."

"Justin would never do something like that. Even if Mr. Samuels ruined his life's dream of working in the surfboard shop."

"Oh," I said casually as I wiped down my counter. "How did he do that?"

She snuffled as if just having to tell the story made her angry. "Justin has been wanting to work in Mayfield Surf Shop ever since he was a little kid. Problem was, no one ever left their position there because it's a cool place to work."

"I'm sure."

"Well, a miracle finally happened, and someone left the shop. They needed a new salesman. Justin would've been perfect for that. He knows a ton about surfboards. He applied for the job. The only reference he had was Mr. Samuels at the theater. And that mean old man told the surf shop owner not to hire Justin. He told him he was unreliable and lazy." Her voice wavered for a second. She quickly rubbed her nose to stop a sniffle. "Justin was really upset, but he would never kill anyone."

I stopped my task. "No, of course not. That wasn't very nice of Mr. Samuels. Don't worry about the investigation. Like I said, Detective Briggs will find out who did it."

Trinity glanced back over her shoulder at her sister. Jazmin was too focused on the bouquet pictures to notice or care about our conversation. Trinity turned back to me. "I think Connie Wilkerson has been trolling the Mayfield Four with bad online reviews. She might be paying people to write terrible one star reviews. There were a whole bunch lately. It was making Mr. Samuels red in the face every time one showed up. He assumed they were legitimate and took it out on all of us. That was why he was yelling at Justin about not cleaning the theaters better between movies. A lot of the reviews complained that the auditoriums were really dirty and that there were rats running around the place."

The last part caught my undivided attention. "Rats? Was there a rat problem?" It was still a puzzle why there was an almost methodically stacked pile of empty rat poison boxes sitting in the trash bin.

"Not that I knew of. No one liked Mr. Samuels but Connie liked him least of all." She seemed to be trying to lay the blame on Connie. I was certain Briggs had her on the list to interview, especially since there had been a rather public ongoing feud between the two theater owners.

"I've got it narrowed down to six bouquets," Jazmin stated proudly from her stool.

Trinity rolled her eyes and looked back at her sister. "Oh my gosh, Jaz. They're just a bunch of flowers. They'll be dead before you open the last wedding gift. Just pick something."

Trinity turned back to me with a satisfied huff. "Justin and I have already decided we're not going through the hassle of a wedding."

I finished cleaning my work counter. "Is that right?"

"Yep. I won't even need one of those expensive dresses. We're going to put on our bathing suits and paddle out past the breakers on our surfboards and get married out on the water. And the only people invited will be people willing to paddle out on boards too."

"So the only flowers will be seaweed." I smiled. "That sounds like a unique wedding indeed."

The bell on the door rang. Trinity's face lit up when she saw that Ryder had returned. He looked calm, so I could easily conclude that there were no ghostly encounters.

"Did you take care of the problem?" I asked.

He was holding back a grin. "Apparently, Shauna had tripped over Bloomer's rawhide chew bone so often she got mad and put it on a shelf in the storage room to get it out of her way."

I laughed. "Bloomer was howling for his rawhide?"

"Seems that way." He shook his head and muttered as he walked past to the office. "Something tells me that won't be my only ghost busting mission this week."

CHAPTER 21

*A*fter a long morning with Jazmin, who finally decided on one of my first bouquet examples with pink peonies and yellow roses, I was more than pleased to meet a certain handsome detective at Franki's Diner for lunch.

Briggs had texted that he'd gotten us a booth in the back, away from the clatter of the kitchen and the busy foot traffic along the counter. Franki spotted me as I walked into the diner. She whirred past me with a large tray of food. "I figured that's why he waited for the booth in the back." She winked. "Lots of privacy for a romantic lunch."

I shook my head. "Not sure how romantic a bowl of chili can be, but I'm sure we'll give it our best." I headed to the back corner of the diner.

Briggs had gone casual, or as casual as his job allowed. He had wisely left his coat and tie behind at the station. There was something extra pleasant about the way his strong forearms looked with the sleeves of his shirt rolled up.

He put down the menu he was holding when he saw me. I

slipped into the booth across from him. He patted the menu. "I don't know why I bother to look. I always order either the burger or the bowl of chili. I'm thinking chili is too hot for this weather."

"I agree. I'm going for the chicken salad sandwich. Nice and refreshing because Franki puts chunks of grapes in it."

"Hmm, that does sound good. Maybe I'll step out of my comfort zone today and try the chicken salad."

I stacked the menus on top of each other. "A few months together and I've turned you into a wild risk taker."

Franki swept over and quickly took our order. She was particularly harried today. The tables and the counter were filled with lunch customers. She pushed a stray hair off her forehead. "This heat wave is great for business. No one wants to turn on a stove at home. But I'm exhausted. I'll be right back with your teas."

I leaned back and relaxed for the first time all morning. "I know Franki insisted this was to be a romantic lunch, but I'm about to change all that by bringing up the investigation. Any word from the coroner?"

"Nothing definitive. Still waiting for the lab results. But Doc Patty," he said the name with the usual hint of mockery, "is still leaning toward poisoning. She managed to get a health history from Samuels' doctor. He was on a lot of different medications for cholesterol, blood pressure and a few other ailments. Doc Patty mentioned that would make him much more vulnerable to poisoning."

"*And* for a possible heart attack," I suggested. "Maybe this wasn't murder after all. Maybe this was just a grumpy man with frail health who worked himself into a lather about something and his heart gave out."

Franki delivered the iced tea. I picked mine right up for a cooling sip.

Briggs reached for a sugar packet. "No, that's been ruled out.

There's a certain enzyme that spikes in the blood after a heart attack. Initial blood tests came back negative."

"Troponin," I stated confidently. He looked properly impressed. "Two years of medical school," I reminded him. I was well on my way to becoming a doctor when my super sensitive nose had other plans. The smells and odors of the anatomy lab were just too much for me. "Then I guess the heart attack theory is put to rest for good."

Briggs stared at his tea in thought as he stirred in the sugar. He had that faraway look in his brown eyes that he got whenever he was trying to puzzle something out.

I sat forward. "Detective Briggs, I can see the gears spinning in your head."

I jarred him out of his thoughts. He smiled and took a drink of tea. "I was just thinking about the conversation I had with Dylan Samuels last night. When I called to tell him that his father had been found dead on his office floor."

"Yes? How did he react?"

"His reaction was what I expected. Shock, despair. He immediately asked how he died. He had to have known with all the medications his dad took that he was a textbook case for a heart attack. He didn't ask if it was his heart. Even we jumped to that conclusion at first and we didn't know his health history." He shook his head. "I'm just grasping at straws." He swirled the straw in his drink and smiled. "Literally and figuratively, it seems."

"I think your speculation is valid. It seemed he lied about his last conversation with his dad. It was more agitated than he first reported. By the way, Trinity, the employee from the theater who poured salt in the machine, came into the shop this morning. I think I mentioned to you that her sister is getting married, and I'm working on her flowers. She told me a couple of things that may or may not be significant. First, she mentioned that Justin, the theater usher, had been trying to land his dream job at the Mayfield Surf Shop. Apparently, it's not easy to get a position there."

Briggs nodded. "Makes sense. Probably a cool place to work if you're a surfer."

"Exactly. Well, a position opened up and Justin applied. But he had to put Mr. Samuels down as his reference."

Briggs nodded. "Let me guess. Samuels gave him a terrible review."

"Yes. It blew Justin's chances. And speaking of reviews, Trinity also mentioned that she thought Connie Wilkerson had been paying people to leave bad reviews online for the Mayfield Four. Including reviews that claim the place is crawling with rats."

Briggs' brow lifted. "Rats? Maybe there was something to all those rat poison boxes in the trash."

"Maybe."

Our chicken salad sandwiches arrived. "Anything else I can get you two?" Franki asked. She looked at us both with a 'how cute is this' smile.

"Nope, I think we're good," I said. "Thanks, Franki."

"You bet."

Briggs watched her walk away. "Why do I get the feeling that our dating has added a whole new topic of conversation to the town's gossip chain?"

I picked up my sandwich. "Because it has. That's only because it's new. Another fresh topic will come around to replace it soon enough." I took a bite and Briggs did the same.

He nodded as he chewed and swallowed. "Good choice."

"What's your next step?" I asked

"I'm going to head over to Connie's house for a chat. If you can get away, I'm going this afternoon. If you'd like to—"

"Yes I would," I said quickly.

He laughed. "You don't even know what I was going to say.

Maybe I was going to say if you'd like to mow my lawn that would be great."

"I know you need *the* nose to snoop about the place. And since Samantha and I come as a team, it was easy to predict what you were going to say. And I've got my own lawn to mow, thanks."

"I guess then the *three* of us will head over to Mayfield after lunch. We have no witnesses that place Connie at the scene, but she does seem to have a motive. In fact, with Mr. Samuels being disliked by so many people, it seems there is no shortage of motives for this murder. Now, if we could just find the person who disliked Samuels the most."

CHAPTER 22

*B*usiness was slow and Ryder had no qualms about running the shop while I took a quick trip to Mayfield. He'd set himself the task of cleaning up all the ribbon spools and reorganizing them for easier use.

Briggs checked the map on his phone. "It's just a half mile ahead." The street we traveled along was quiet with nicely kept houses. A bright blue Toyota zipped past us. We both happened to glance at the driver as she drove past. Briggs looked quickly over at me. "Was that Sally Applegate?"

"I was just about to ask you the same thing. Now that I think about it, I did see a bright blue Toyota just like that in the theater parking lot. It's a striking color. Easy to remember. It must have been her. Do you think she was coming from Connie's house?"

"Unless she happens to live on the same street, that would be my guess."

"Maybe she's trying to find a new job and she's hoping Connie can finally afford to take her on," I suggested.

"That doesn't sound too farfetched." Briggs turned right at a small dead-end street called Clover Road. He parked under a massive poplar tree to keep the car cool. There was no car parked on the driveway in front of Connie's house, a cute pale green bungalow with white trim and a jutting front porch.

"Do you think she's home?" I asked.

"Guess we'll find out." We walked up the driveway.

There was no way for my nose to ignore the warm, penetrating smell of a car engine hovering over the empty driveway. "She might not be home, but I'm certain there was a car sitting in this driveway just moments ago."

We climbed the porch steps. A hand painted welcome sign that was covered with stars greeted us on the front door. Briggs knocked. It opened quickly, almost as if Connie was expecting someone. Or maybe she thought her previous guest had forgotten something.

"Detective Briggs," she said with a good degree of surprise.

"Miss Wilkerson," Briggs said with a nod. "This is my assistant, Miss Pinkerton. May we come in? I'd like to ask you a few questions."

Connie Wilkerson was forty something. Her white summery dress was covered in yellow polka dots. Her short reddish-brown hair was pushed back with a matching polka dot headband. I could smell onions, tomatoes and basil drifting out from the kitchen as we stepped into the house. An overhead fan was spinning at top speed, pushing mostly hot air around.

She stopped in the center of the front room. The walls were decorated with framed classic movie posters, including one from Casablanca. "What can I do for you, Detective Briggs?"

Briggs didn't pull out his notebook right away. I'd seen him delay it whenever he didn't want to put someone on defense before he even got started. "Miss Wilkerson, I'm sure by now you've heard the news about Ronald Samuels."

"Yes, I have and I can't say I'm sad or upset. I know that sounds callous, but that's how I feel. I never lie."

Briggs cleared his throat. "Yes, I understand. I know there had been some tension between the two of you."

Her nostrils flared in indignation at his mild statement. "Some tension? The man set my theater on fire. I nearly lost everything because of him." It seemed to dawn on her that the show of anger wasn't the best way to present herself to the man investigating Samuels' murder. She relaxed and dropped her chin. "Of course, I would never resort to anything so heinous as murder." She shot a curious look my direction. I smiled politely in return. What I needed was to find a way to get into the garage to sniff for coolant. Even that was probably going to prove worthless because if coolant had been the culprit, then the murderer had access to it at the theater.

My sniffer did help me devise a way to bring up Sally Applegate. "Did you and Sally make pasta for lunch? It smells delicious. I'm a big fan of basil."

My simple, innocuous question threw her off guard. She stumbled over a few syllables before deciding on an answer. "Sal—Sally who? I'm cooking some spaghetti sauce for dinner."

Briggs stepped right up to bat. "So Sally Applegate didn't leave here a few minutes ago?"

"Sally Applegate?" She placed her hand on her chest for effect. "Why would she be here? As I said, I've been cooking spaghetti sauce."

Briggs casually pulled out his notebook. Connie shifted on her sandals. The movement and the jet engine speed fan above caused the flouncy skirt of her dress to flutter up. Her cheeks darkened as she pushed it quickly down.

"Cute dress," I noted. "You're daring cooking spaghetti sauce in a white dress."

Briggs snuck a sideways peek at me. He knew too well that I

was pointing that fact out to him, a man, someone who might not notice that a white and yellow polka dot dress was hardly practical for cooking with tomatoes.

"I was wearing an apron," she said crisply. "Can we hurry this along, Detective Briggs? I need to get ready for work."

"Just a few more questions. I'll make it fast. I'm sure your theater will be extra crowded tonight since the Mayfield Four is closed."

Her brows rose with an innocent blink. "Oh wow, I hadn't even considered that possibility."

Her statement about never lying seemed to be what one might refer to as a lie. Especially because I was convinced Sally's car had been in the driveway just seconds before our arrival. No other cars had passed us, so unless a neighbor had driven over parked in the driveway and driven right back home, it had to be Sally.

"Miss Wilkerson." Briggs flipped open his notebook. "Can you tell me where you were last night between the hours of seven and nine?"

"Yes, of course," she said and then paused. "I arrived at the Starlight at noon to help with the matinees."

"So you were there all afternoon and night, until closing?" he asked.

"No, actually, I stayed until almost six to do some paperwork and make sure the evening shows went off without a hitch. Then I came back home for a few hours to eat dinner and rest before heading back at ten to help clean and close up."

He wrote down some notes. "What time was that dinner break at home?"

"I think I got home around six and I was here until half past nine. I remember because I was just getting into my car when the phone rang. My ticket manager called to let me know about Mr. Samuels' death."

"I see. Did you have company or were you alone?"

She laughed dryly. "Alone. I'm hardly in the mood to entertain during my few hours of rest."

Briggs looked up from his notebook. "Is there anyone who can confirm you were here? A neighbor who saw your car in the driveway?"

Her face turned smooth and pale. "Certainly I'm not being considered a suspect. I was here those hours. I made myself a tuna sandwich and sat with my book right there on the couch. Right below the Gone with the Wind poster. I can ask neighbors if they saw me pull into the driveway, but I always park in the garage."

Briggs lowered his pen. "Is it possible to see the garage?" He'd read my mind.

It seemed as if she was going to deny his request at first. Her shoulders had grown more rigid, and her chin jutted forward in defense. "Yes, I have nothing to hide, so by all means. Right this way." She led us to a door in the kitchen that led out to an attached garage.

A white Chevy sedan was parked in the center of the garage. A washer and dryer took up one top corner. One wall was lined with boxes that were labeled for seasonal decorations like Halloween and Christmas. Shelves on the opposite side contained floor cleaner solution, a box of tools and gardening supplies. At the end of the bottom shelf there were at least ten bags of brown pellets. Something told me they were peanut butter flavored rat bait.

Briggs walked over and touched the center of the hood on Connie's car. "You're certain that Sally Applegate wasn't here earlier?" The question stunned Connie.

"Yes, I think I would know if I had a visitor."

"There was the smell of a car motor lingering on your driveway when we walked up," he said plainly.

She fidgeted enough to assure both of us that she'd been caught in a lie. "I went out for a moment. To buy some basil," she added to give weight to her story.

"Except your car is cold," Briggs said.

Her shoulders relaxed with a long groan of surrender. "Fine. Sally was here. We celebrated Mr. Samuels' demise with a pasta lunch. Nobody is sad that man is dead. I can tell you that with confidence."

Briggs glanced around the room casually, but I knew he was calculating and planning his next words. He turned back to her. "Why did you lie about Sally being here?"

"Isn't your being here enough to explain it? I didn't want you to start coming up with some crazy farfetched theory that Sally and I had conspired together to kill Samuels. I didn't want to raise any suspicions."

"Lying to an officer is never a good way to avoid raising suspicions. And no matter what your feelings about the man, a celebratory lunch just hours after his death is a little much. Don't you think?" Briggs asked.

She smoothed her hand primly down the skirt of her dress. "If that's all, I need to get ready for work."

I walked an extra wide berth around the car to sniff the bags of pellets on the shelf. It was an artificial smell that mimicked peanut butter. "Do these work?" My question bounced around the tension in the garage and landed squarely Connie.

She blinked in confusion at me.

"The peanut butter flavored rat bait? Does it work?" I repeated.

Briggs' eyes flashed toward the bags as I spoke.

I picked up a bag and examined it. "Does it take care of the rat problem? I've noticed some of them are chewing the boxes in my garage."

"Uh, I—I'm not sure." She stuttered over her answer. "I mean I haven't tried it yet."

"I see." I smiled mildly at Briggs. "Are we through here, Detective Briggs? It seems we're keeping Miss Wilkerson from her busy night at the theater."

"Yes. Thank you for your time."

Connie hit a button to lift the garage door to show us a faster way out.

CHAPTER 23

Since I'd taken an extra break from the shop to visit Connie Wilkerson with Briggs, I gave Ryder the rest of the afternoon off. Business was so slow I contemplated closing up early. I couldn't blame the entire slump on the heat wave. It was my first year as a florist. I was slowly seeing trends and peaks and valleys in business. Most of it was connected to the time of year. Holidays were booming, along with early spring when most of the wedding orders came in. Jazmin was my only bridal customer at the moment, but I expected more orders near Christmas. Winter weddings were growing in popularity. But the end of summer was a time when people were using their extra cash for back to school items and last minute vacations. Flowers were probably an unnecessary expense. Wisely, I'd learned to save during peak seasons and scrimp during the valleys.

I'd finished up purchase orders, reorganized my office and found myself with time to think about the murder investigation. Briggs had driven back to Port Danby deep in thought. We'd both agreed that Connie's behavior and the lie about Sally, along with her outright disdain for Samuels, put her in the person of interest category. In fact, the piles of unused rat poison and her general lack of a good alibi had moved her higher on that list. The question that remained was how could Connie have poisoned the slush without anyone seeing her? Certainly, given her reputation as Samuels' vocal enemy, theater workers would have noticed Connie Wilkerson walking through the Mayfield Four. It seemed far more plausible that the murderer had been inside the theater all along.

Kingston's nemesis, the pushy mockingbird, had flown off earlier in the day. My crow had found enough courage to take a tour around the neighborhood. He'd been gone a good hour, so I walked outside to look for him.

The blast of hot air I expected was followed by a gentle coastal breeze. It seemed the worst was over. We were headed back to being a coastal town with beachy weather rather than a town that had somehow been dropped onto the surface of planet Mercury.

I shaded my eyes and scanned the sky and the trees, but there was no sign of Kingston.

"Lacey," a voice called from across the street. Shauna glanced both directions quickly before hurrying over to my side. She looked frantically into the shop window. "Is Ryder around? I think there's something or someone in the attic of the shop. I can hear footsteps, like someone is moving something around." She didn't wait for my response and rushed past me to the front door.

"Ryder is off for the afternoon."

She froze with one foot inside the shop, then turned around and joined me on the sidewalk. "What will I do? I can't possibly go back inside that store. What if it's a ghost or an ax murderer?"

"Or a ghost who is also an ax murderer," I chided.

Her lips puckered in displeasure. "This isn't funny. Can you call Ryder for me?"

"No, it's not funny. I'm sorry. I'll walk over to the antique shop with you and see if I can find out what's going on."

Her disappointment in not having Ryder come to her rescue was palpable. It seemed a good fright was much more fun when there was a handsome knight to come to your rescue, instead of a curly haired, sarcastic flower shop owner.

I locked my shop door and took one last sky survey for my bird before walking nervous Shauna back to the antique store. It was easy to see why she needed an anxiety support group. That thought pushed an idea into my head. After I solved the ax murderer problem, I hoped to grill her a bit on her group mate, Sally. I hadn't considered Sally a person of interest until the strange incident at Connie's.

Shauna stopped a foot back from the door with a frightful gaze as if something might jump out at us from inside. I was sure going to have a few good stories to tell Lola when she returned. I wondered if she realized that her humble little antique shop was a favorite hot spot for menacing spirits.

"I'll go in first," I suggested, but there seemed to be no question about it. Late Bloomer lifted his head from his pillow as we walked back inside. The ghost didn't seem to have Lola's dog too agitated.

Shauna stood plastered to the door. Her eyes darting back and forth, again waiting for something to jump out at her. I patted Bloomer on the head. I might have been imagining it, but I could have almost sworn the dog shot me a secret eye roll.

"Where did you hear the sound?"

Shauna finally peeled herself off the door, her emergency escape hatch, apparently, and tiptoed toward me. Her shoulders were up around her ears as she peered cautiously up at the ceiling. She was just halfway when a quick succession of taps was followed by a rolling sound. Before I could peel my gaze from the noisy ceiling, Shauna was outside the door, hugging herself and pacing the sidewalk.

I listened again. After a few seconds of silence, the tapping sound continued. Once again a strange rolling sound followed. Naturally, with the day I'd had, my mind went right to rats. I knew Lola was vigilant about pests in her shop. A rat could cause catastrophic damage to antiques.

Shauna was at the door now, staring in with eyes as wide as saucers, waiting for her volunteer ghost buster to get to work. Lola had a ladder in the storage room. The small attic door was in the same room. I didn't relish the idea of having to climb up into the dark, cluttered space above the store, but if I didn't determine the source of the noise, there was no way Shauna would ever step foot inside the antique store again.

I headed along the short hallway to the storage room. As I reached for the door, a tapping sound skittered across the ceiling. It sounded vaguely familiar. I waited for it again. Titter tatter, titter tatter. My laugh was stifled in the narrow passage. It was a sound I'd heard far too often.

I headed outside. Shauna stepped away from the door as I opened it. She was white as the sidewalk below her fidgety feet. "Did you see anything?" she asked.

"Not yet." I walked out to the middle of Harbor Lane and got up on tiptoes to get a view of the roof. The menacing ghostly culprit appeared, only he was far from ghostly and only slightly menacing. Kingston saw me standing on the sidewalk below and dropped the shelled walnut he was holding in his beak. The nut rolled quickly down the roof. My crow titter tattered after it.

Shauna looked baffled. "Is that Kingston?"

"Yes, and I'm afraid he's the one making the noise on the roof. It seems he found a walnut and carried it up to Lola's roof to eat. Only the pitch of the roof seems to be making that task difficult."

Shauna released a long breath. "Thank goodness. I was sure something terrible was lurking up in the attic. Are you sure it was Kingston making the sounds?"

"Yes, I recognized his footsteps pretty quickly." I whistled for Kingston to come down. He picked up the walnut and flew across the street to the roof of the flower shop.

"I'll walk back in with you to make sure the problem is gone, but I'm sure the tapping noise just flew over to my side of Harbor Lane. Shauna was still tense about walking inside the shop. I decided to get her mind off the earlier scare.

"Have you heard from Lola?" I asked. "Is she having a good time?"

Shauna's steps lightened as she followed me across to the counter. "She seems to be having a good time, but it's always hard to tell with Lo-lo. She can be a little sarcastic."

"Who? Lola?" I said with a chuckle. "I'm sure she's having fun. I mean it's France."

"Well, thanks for figuring out the sound. So Ryder isn't coming back for the rest of the day?" she asked casually as if it was just an afterthought. (Which it clearly wasn't.)

"I don't expect to see him again until morning. He watched the shop for me while I went on an errand. I was going to ask you—you mentioned that Sally Applegate, the assistant manager at the theater, was in your anxiety support group."

She gasped slightly. "My mom said the theater manager died right in the middle of a movie. Just dropped dead in front of the audience."

Lola had mentioned her Aunt Ruby liked to put her own spin on things. It seemed she was right. "No, that isn't exactly how it happened. He was in his office. No audience." I pulled her back to the original topic. "Do you know Sally well?"

"Not really. She's about ten years older than me, so it wasn't like we hung out or anything." Shauna walked around to the other side of the counter and picked up the bottle of glass cleaner and the rag she had sitting near the register. "Mostly what I know about her is what she's talked about at group."

"I see. Well, I guess that kind of information has to be kept in the group." I looked expectantly at her, hoping she'd still drop a few tidbits. I was in luck.

"We're not really supposed to talk about stuff outside of group, but I'm thinking of quitting so I guess that rule doesn't apply anymore."

"You're not going to group anymore?"

"Nah, I don't really need it." It seemed she'd entirely wiped away the last half hour from her memory. "But I can tell you, Sally is a good candidate for the group. She has so much stress in her life. Poor lady."

I inched closer to the counter and tried to contain my enthusiasm for hearing more. "Stress?" I asked lightly. "What kind of stress?"

She sprayed the cleaning fluid on the glass top of the counter. I rubbed my nose to stop it from twitching into a massive sneeze.

"The usual kind of stuff," she continued as she wiped the glass. "She was struggling to pay her bills. Her mom is sick with some kind of nerve thing. I guess the doctors don't know what it is but she's always in bed. Sally is taking care of her and trying to make sure her mom doesn't lose the house. Then there is the stress of working for that awful boss of hers." She looked up wide-eyed from her task. "I guess that stress has been removed now."

"Yes but a new one has sprung up," I noted. "Sally might not have a job if the theater closes down."

"I hadn't thought of that. But they'll open it again. The Mayfield Four is way nicer than the Starlight."

"Do you think so?"

"Everyone thinks so," she said confidently.

I patted Late Bloomer's head again. He didn't stir from his nap. "I better go open up for Kingston to get to his perch. He's probably worked himself into a lather trying to break open the nut. Sorry he gave you a fright," I said on my way out.

"He didn't give me a fright."

Yep, she'd definitely forgotten the entire last half hour.

CHAPTER 24

*M*y chat with Shauna sparked my interest in the online reviews for the Mayfield Four Theater. Trinity was sure Connie had paid people to leave bad reviews.

I opened up the shop and Kingston swooped past me. The walnut was still wedged in his beak. He flew to his perch, holding tight to his prize. The second I picked up his treat can, with goodies that took much less effort to eat, he dropped the walnut. It fell onto the tray beneath his perch. While he was busy eating his treats, I grabbed the nut, carried it to the work island and used the handle end of a screwdriver to crack it open. I dug out the nut meats and carried them back to the perch.

"Here," I said. "And let's just be glad your mockingbird friend wasn't around to witness that sad display of bird-ness."

I headed into the office and sat down at the computer. Mayfield Four had over a hundred reviews with an average of three stars. It seemed ratings were either five or one, with very little in between, which, frankly, made both sides a little suspect. For me to give a five star rating to a regular old neighborhood theater, I'd expect the seat to recline like my dad's easy chair and gourmet snacks to be served by the movie stars themselves. Some of the rave reviews seemed to indicate that my wish list had just about been met, sans food delivery by movie stars. Comfortable seating, attentive staff and great sound system were among the things complimented. But there were plenty of negative reviews too. One person's entire review complained about there being far too many unpopped kernels in their bucket of popcorn.

I scrolled down to some of the more recent reviews, in particular, the one stars. Some stated plainly that the theater was disgustingly dirty. One reviewer went so far as to post a picture. I clicked on the review, and it opened up wider. Interestingly enough, it was a photo of a stack of rat poison boxes sitting in the trash bin. The reviewer who called themselves Mary J. wrote— "enter this theater at your own risk. They have a rat infestation. Just look at this trash bin behind the theater. I think I'll spend my movie money at the Starlight up the street instead. At least that theater isn't crawling with rodents".

It was just a touch too obvious to include a comparison of a competing theater. It seemed Trinity was right about Connie possibly paying people to write bad reviews of the Mayfield Four. Only, after finding the evidence sitting right in view in Connie's garage, I'd say the staged photo of the rat poison and one star review that came with it was posted by Connie herself.

CHAPTER 25

I finished my review search and was shutting down the computer for the evening when Elsie's sing song voice was followed by a delicious aroma. A mix of butter and brown sugar, according to my infallible nose.

"Yoo hoo, Pink," she called. "I've got cookies."

My chair rolled across the floor as I leapt out of it at the word *cookies*.

Elsie was standing at the island with a plate of goodies and one of her mini handheld fans. "I come bearing gifts."

"You know I love all of your gifts." She handed me the plate and the fan. "Why are you handing me this? Don't your customers need it? I saw a few of them holding them in front of their faces while they nibbled baked goods."

"Turns out they aren't a very efficient way to keep my customers cool. I had to keep replacing the batteries. I'm giving up on them. Batteries are way too expensive. It'd be cheaper to hire people to stand with giant ostrich feather fans and wave them at the customers."

I decided not to bring up Lester's gigantic fan. I didn't need to *fan* the flames of sibling rivalry between my two neighbors. I put the plate on the counter. The cookies were filled with everything from bits of chocolate and nuts to chopped cranberries.

I picked one up and bit it. It was a mix of flavors all wrapped in a buttery, brown sugar cookie. "Hmm, very good. What are they called?"

"I call them Clutter Cookies. I make them whenever I decide to clean out the clutter in my bakery pantry. It's a nice way to get rid of half used bags of chocolate and nuts and fruits. The cookie is just a basic chocolate chip dough recipe."

I swallowed another bite. "There is nothing basic about anything you bake, Elsie." I picked up a second cookie and turned it back and forth to admire it. "Clutter Cookies. A new favorite."

Elsie climbed up on a stool. "So what's with the murder at the theater? I assume a certain charismatic detective is on the case."

"Gosh, that's right. I haven't talked to you since our movie date."

Elsie spun on the stool to watch me as I grabbed the watering pot to give the plants in the front window a drink. "Were you two at the theater when Ronald Samuels died?"

"Yep, right in the middle of Casablanca. They pulled James out of the movie. Poor guy. Even when he has the night off, he's still on duty. At least in everyone else's eyes." I leaned into the window area and poured the water.

"I went to city college with Ronald Samuels," Elsie said. "That was forty years ago, but I can tell you he was as unlikeable then as he was now. Always grumpy."

I straightened from the window and walked back to the island with the watering pot. "Interesting. I had no idea you knew him."

"Not well. He wasn't exactly the kind of person you wanted to befriend. Still, it's sad that he died," she added with a touch of sincerity. "I hear he dropped right in front of one of his audiences. Poison?"

"He died alone in his office. Boy, rumors sure do get big and swirly in this town. Looks like poison. Normally that detail wouldn't be out yet but the new coroner, Doc Patty, as she prefers to be called, sort of announced her findings to all the employees. It always makes James' job that much harder when crucial details are leaked out."

"Yes, that makes sense. From what I've heard, Connie Wilkerson of the Starlight Theater has been in a feud with the man. Especially after he set fire to her place."

"That was never proven, and I seriously doubt Samuels would have taken the risk. His theater does far better business."

"I suppose that's true. Connie has tried hard to make a go of it with the Starlight, but she just never seemed to gain traction. She comes into my bakery every Thursday for a peach muffin, and I always have to hear her long list of problems."

"Does she?"

"Nine in the morning. Like clockwork. Unless she's too busy now with overflow business from the Mayfield Four."

"I might just drop casually by tomorrow while she's buying her muffin. There's a few things I want to ask her."

CHAPTER 26

*K*ingston decided to take advantage of the early evening cool down. He took off over the town and headed toward the Pickford Lighthouse. The tall trees that bordered the west side of town were always a hangout for other crows. I sometimes fretted like a worried mother that he didn't have enough friends, or at least friends that weren't human. He never mingled with the other crows much. He just led way too different of a life, but occasionally, he liked to perch nearby the crows. Kind of like the outcast sitting near the popular kids, wanting to be one of the gang. That thought often saddened me and made me wonder if I was doing the wrong thing keeping him domestic. I was sure he'd have a terrible time trying to adapt to the wild. He was just too set in his ways. And, selfish as it seemed, I was too used to having him around.

Briggs' car was out front of the police station. A visit with my favorite detective would be a great way to fill the time while I waited for Kingston to get the call of the wild out of his blood for the night.

Hilda was just cleaning up her desk at the front counter as I walked inside. "Hello, Lacey," she chirped. "Perfect timing. He just got back." She buzzed me in and swept past me with her purse. "Have a good night."

"You too, Hilda." I knocked on the office door and poked my head in as he called good night to Hilda. "It's me. Are you busy?"

His white teeth sparkled. "Never too busy for you."

I sashayed in. "I can remember a time when Miss Pinkerton's unexpected visit was considered a nuisance."

"No, never a nuisance."

I stood over his desk and stared at him.

"O.K. maybe a tiny bit of a nuisance. But that was before I discovered that the highly curious Miss Pinkerton and her turbo charged sense of smell were brilliant at solving crimes."

I sat down. "Brilliant, huh? I like that word. Really captures my essence." I leaned forward and rested my forearms along the edge of his desk. He had his notebook out and was transcribing some of it onto the computer.

"I found out a few things of interest," he said.

"Me too."

He leaned back. "You first."

His wonderful brown eyes stole my breath for a brief second. "Uh yes, all right." It took me a moment to remember what I was going to tell him. "First of all, and this is just sort of a side note about the victim's character. More affirmation that Mr. Samuels was unpleasant and not well liked. Elsie told me she went to city college at the same time as him, and even back then, in his twenties, he was a grumpy, disagreeable sort. I know that doesn't push the case forward, but I thought I'd mention it. Also, I decided to check out the reviews for the Mayfield Four Theater. Remember when I told you, Trinity seemed to think Connie was using online reviews to sabotage Samuels?"

"Yes, right." Briggs peeled a note off the bottom of his monitor. "Had a note to do just that. What did you find?"

"People either loved the Mayfield Four or they hated it. There were few in between reviews. Which leads me to believe that while Connie was paying people to write bad reviews, Samuels was paying people to write good ones. Although, I could be totally wrong about both assumptions. However, there was one reviewer, a person who called themselves Mary J., who took the time to post a picture to give weight to her assertion that the Mayfield Four was infested with rats."

Briggs' chair squeaked as he sat forward with interest. "Was it a picture of rats?"

"Not quite. Remember that nicely stacked set of poison boxes in the trash bin?"

His forehead relaxed. "So Connie Wilkerson bought the poison to stage a picture that went with her infestation claim." He tilted his head side to side. "Elaborate but I guess if you're going after your enemy, you have to be crafty. Of course, posting a staged photo of rat poison doesn't mean the next step is murder. But it does show just how far she was willing to go to hurt Samuels."

"Not only that," I said, "but I keep inadvertently making the connection between the rat poison and the method used to kill Samuels. What if Connie bought the poison and hoped to also use it to kill Samuels. It has a peanut butter flavor. Maybe she was conspiring with Sally to somehow get it into his food."

"Possible but probably farfetched. Those pellets might trick a rat into thinking its eating peanut butter, but I doubt it tastes anything like the real thing."

I shrugged. "Just a theory."

"And a good one. I'll keep it in mind."

"What did you find out today in your detective adventures?"

His chuckle was always pleasant to hear. "My adventures took me to the hospital."

I nearly popped off my chair. "What? Why?"

"I guess I phrased that badly. I went to visit the ex Mrs. Samuels. I called ahead and the doctor told me I could see her for ten minutes to ask a few questions as long as I didn't upset her."

"How was she doing? Still recovering from the shock?" I asked.

"She didn't seem to be shocked or sad. She was weak, of course, from surgery and hooked up to a lot of machines, but it seemed she wasn't the slightest bit upset that her ex-husband was dead."

"I guess that falls in line with most people's reactions." I shifted back in the chair. "But it doesn't fall in line with what Dylan Samuels told you regarding their argument."

Briggs pointed and winked. "Bingo. She practically laughed when I asked her if she was upset that her ex-husband never came to visit her in the hospital. Dylan insisted she was hoping to see him. But she told me that would have only sent her right into cardiac arrest. She says she can't stand the sight of him. She blamed her heart disease on the stress of living under his constant verbal abuse for twenty-five years."

"I wonder why she stuck it out so long," I said.

"Who knows? Maybe it was because of Dylan. Which brings me to one last detail. Since Virginia, that's her name, wasn't feeling too distraught over the death, I brought up Mr. Samuels' will. It didn't seem too impertinent, given that she didn't seem the slightest bit emotional about the murder. And that gave me another clue as to why she could have cared less about his death. As could be expected, she was no longer one of his beneficiaries, but apparently, neither was Dylan."

My eyes rounded. "His only son was not a beneficiary?"

"Nope. According to Virginia, Samuels changed his will a year ago and left everything, including the theater, to an unknown beneficiary. The lawyer has the document, so she and Dylan are left in the dark about who will inherit his money and theater. I put a call into the lawyer to find out if and when the name can be made public."

"I guess that Dylan Samuels doesn't have a money motive then."

"My thoughts exactly." He reached his arm out across the desk, and I happily placed my hand in his. "I thought we could have dinner tonight."

"I like that idea, only I defrosted a dish of lasagna my mom left in the freezer for me on her visit. I have to eat it or it will get mushy. Why don't you come over. Technically, my mom's cooking, and she's way better at it than me."

"Sounds good. I'll be another hour or so." He got back to his notebook.

"And I have to round up my bird, so that works out perfectly."

CHAPTER 27

The aroma of my mom's cheesy, tomato filled lasagna circled the kitchen, making me hungry and homesick all at the same time. That crafty woman knew just what she was doing when she prepared and froze some of her best homemade dishes for me to heat long after she and Dad had gone home. If I'd had a spare moment, I would have called to let her know I was on to her culinary scheme. But as it was, I was scurrying around getting dressed and ready for my dinner date.

After I left the police station, I walked back toward the flower shop to pick up my car. I drove to the town square to look for Kingston. He was sitting with a group of crows that had pulled a bag with French fries out of a trash can. Again, like the mom of a kid who didn't always fit in, I hung back and let him be a crow for a few more minutes without the embarrassment of having mommy tell him it was time to come in for the night. I started to feel just a touch hurt that he was ignoring me, but the second the last fry was gone, he flew toward the car with hardly a glance back at his new friends. Apparently, it had been more about the French fries than the buddies.

I opened every window in the house to get a fresh breeze flowing through the rooms. More moderate coastal temperatures were returning, and I welcomed the salty, cool air. I dashed into the bathroom once more to check my lipstick when a knock sounded on the front door.

It had only been an hour since I saw Briggs but a smattering of butterflies took a quick tour around my stomach. I hurried to the door and opened it.

Dash was standing on the front porch with a pickle jar in his left hand and his right hand pasted to his side. "Yes, I understand the irony of this scene, but I need help getting the jar open. I'm trying to make a sandwich, and in order for it to be a success, it requires a pickle."

I laughed. "Of course it does." I lifted my arm and curled it to reveal a terribly unimpressive bicep. "You came to the right person," I said in a deep voice. With no small degree of confidence, I took hold of the jar and gave it a good twist. I added in a manly grunt, which fell hilariously flat when I realized I hadn't budged the thing. "Or maybe you didn't come to the right person. But you're in luck. I have faced down a stubborn jar on more than one occasion and I have another trick up my sleeve." I motioned for him to follow me into the house to keep the moths fluttering around the porch light from flying inside.

I carried the jar into the kitchen and pulled out the can opener to pry the lid and release the vacuum.

Dash took a deep breath. "Smells good." He glanced around at my spotless kitchen. "You are a very tidy cook."

"No, actually, I'm the opposite of tidy. This was a prebaked lasagna my mom made. My only part in it was putting it in the oven to heat."

Dash noticed the two place settings on my table. "I guess you're expecting Briggs." He took hold of the jar. "I will take my pickles and get out of your way. Thank you, by the way. This injury has hurt my masculine pride far more than it's hurt my broken shoulder. Hopefully, the pickle jar is the low point and things will look up after this."

"I think it takes a man comfortable in his own skin to admit when he needs help with a pickle jar."

"Maybe I'm being too hard on myself," he said with a chuckle.

I reached for the door and opened it for him. Pickle jar in hand, he stopped suddenly as if someone had glued his feet to the floor.

"Briggs," he said quietly.

I peered around the edge of the door. Briggs looked at me before facing Dash.

"Vanhouten," he said. If not for the fact that it seemed to come from between clenched teeth, it almost sounded polite.

Coward that I was, I stayed mostly behind the door, using it as a shield of sorts.

Dash held up the jar. "Turns out pickle jars are hard to open with one hand."

"Yes, I heard about your accident. Hope you're feeling better," Briggs said.

I sucked in an audible breath and quickly covered my mouth to stifle it.

"Thanks. Not sure what I would have done if Lacey hadn't been kind enough to drive me to the hospital." They continued their amicable conversation over my front door threshold. I held my breath hoping, against all odds, it didn't crumble into an argument.

"Yes, it's a good thing." There was a hint of sarcasm in Briggs' words, but I was still giddy at the overall tone of their talk. I wanted nothing more than for Briggs and Dash to be civil with each other. I never expected their old friendship to bloom again. Far too much damage had been done by Dash's selfish behavior, but it would be wonderful not to have to worry about bringing up Dash in conversation.

"I'm friends with Tim Rogers at the coast guard. He mentioned you flew one of the search planes when a pleasure boat went missing," Briggs said. "He said you located the boat even in dense fog. Nice job."

A small squeak came from my throat before I could stop it.

"Lacey, are you going to hide behind the door all night making little sounds?" Briggs called from his side of the threshold.

Dash stepped aside to make room for me to emerge from behind the door. I knew my smile was ear to ear but I didn't mind. "I was having too much fun listening to the conversation. I didn't want to spoil it." I looked up at Dash. "You never told me about the boat rescue. That's wonderful, Dash."

Dash smiled weakly. "It was no big deal. Anyhow, I'll let you two eat dinner. Thanks again for opening the pickles."

Dash nodded at Briggs as he slipped past.

Briggs stepped inside and I shut the door. I spun around on my heels and kissed him.

"Nice appetizer before dinner," he said. "What did I do to deserve such a nice welcome kiss?" The twinkle in his eyes assured me he knew exactly how he'd earned the kiss.

I hopped on my toes and kissed him once more. "Thank you, James."

CHAPTER 28

$\mathcal{I}$ got to work early to finish a few things before my unofficial stake out at Elsie's bakery. It was perfectly plausible that the neighboring shop owner might be sitting at one of Elsie's outdoor tables eating an apricot scone. Plus it gave me an excuse to eat an apricot scone. Elsie's were a splendidly flaky adventure with just the right balance of sweet and tart.

"Heading next door for an apricot scone," I called to Ryder as he washed his hands in the work area. "Do you want anything from Elsie's?"

"No, thanks. My mom made a big breakfast this morning."

"I won't be long."

It was early but a few people were sitting at Elsie's tables, sipping Les's coffee and eating pastries. I didn't see Connie Wilkerson but it was only just nine. And then there was the possibility that she was too busy for a peach muffin now that the Starlight was the only movie venue in Mayfield.

I stepped into the bakery and was instantly lightheaded from the hurricane of delicious aromas swirling around the shop. I had to concentrate not to get overwhelmed by the incredible mix of smells. Customers with regular noses, or noses of this world as my dad liked to say, were treated to the usual charming mix of butter, cinnamon, sugar frosting and fruity scents, but I had to work hard to not *drink* it all in at once.

Elsie finished up with the customers at the counter and waited for them to walk out before greeting me. "Did you come here for an apricot scone fix or for detective work?"

"Both," I said cheerily.

Elsie walked to the end of the counter with the scones and pulled out a golden scone that was dotted with chewy chunks of apricot. "This will probably be the last batch for the summer. Fresh apricots are getting harder to find."

"That's sad to hear but I'm sure you'll find something tasty to replace them." I glanced back toward the sidewalk tables. "No sign of your peach muffin customer yet?"

Elsie glanced up at the clock on the wall. "Huh, not yet. She's late. Maybe she's too busy." She placed the scone on a paper plate and handed it to me. "You sure look extra pink cheeked and happy this morning. Anything I should know about?" She looked pointedly at my left hand.

"If you're looking for an engagement ring, *Mom*, I mean Elsie, we've only been officially dating for five weeks. Might be a little soon for a ring."

"So why the skippy walk and pink apple cheeks this morning?" she asked.

I broke off a corner of the scone. "James and I had a nice dinner last night. My mom's lasagna. My freezer is filled with several husband winning casseroles. She pretended she was doing it because she thought I wasn't eating enough home cooked meals, but she had an ulterior motive. She's still old-fashioned enough to think the best way to a man's heart is through his stomach. Unless I'm doing the cooking." I took a bite of scone.

Elsie laughed. "How is your mom?"

"Great. She and my dad are going on a cruise next week."

The door opened behind me. Elsie smiled. "Morning, Connie."

A crumb of scone stuck in my throat. I covered my mouth and cleared it as Connie approached the counter. She looked my direction and forced a smile. She didn't seem thrilled to see me.

"Morning," I said brightly and held up my scone. "Nothing like one of Elsie's treats to get the day started."

Elsie didn't bother to ask Connie her order and, instead, headed over to the glass case and pulled out a plump peach muffin topped with cinnamon streusel. Connie's somewhat cold expression left me searching for a polite way to change topics to the murder investigation. I didn't want to upset one of Elsie's customers right inside the bakery, so I held my tongue.

Connie paid for her muffin. Elsie had given it to her on a plate. With any luck, she'd eat it outside at the tables. The heat had mellowed enough to allow for it. She walked out.

Elsie whispered behind me. "I think your interrogation suspect just escaped. She usually sits at the corner table."

"I didn't want to do anything that left a bitter taste in her mouth while she was standing inside your bakery." I turned back to her. "I'll talk to you later. I might still have a chance to get in a question, but I have to be stealthy and clever. I went with Briggs to her house, and she wasn't terribly pleased to talk to him about the murder."

I picked up the rest of my scone.

"Have you heard from Lola?" she asked before I walked out.

"No, but next time she leaves she might have to rethink hiring her cousin, Shauna. The poor girl is a nervous wreck. She seems to think the store is haunted. She might very well be over at the flower shop right now convincing Ryder to come check out a floor creak or unexplained moan."

159

"Maybe she just likes to find excuses to have Ryder come to her rescue," Elsie suggested.

"Yes, you and I think alike, my friend. See you later."

I made a point of walking past the corner table where Connie had sat to eat her muffin. She was looking at her phone, which ruined my chances for another conversation. But luck was on my side.

"Is Detective Briggs in his office this morning?" she asked during my slow motion journey between the tables.

I took it as an invite to move closer to the table. "Yes, he should be." I lingered after my answer, hoping there would be more. Luck again. Maybe the apricot scone was my rabbit's foot.

"I've found someone to verify that I was at home during the hours when Samuels was killed. I was so flustered when he questioned me, I completely forgot that the neighbor boy came by just before eight with raffle tickets for his football team. I'm going to let the detective know so he can check me off his list of suspects." She blinked up at me from behind blue framed sunglasses. "I assume I was on the list." She was waiting for affirmation, but it wasn't mine to give.

"You'll have to ask Detective Briggs about that." Since she had opened the discussion, I decided it wouldn't hurt to bring up the reviews. "I was reading through some of the online reviews for the Mayfield Four. According to one review, Mr. Samuels was having a problem with rat infestation. The person took the time to post a picture of some boxes of rat poison in the bin outside the theater." She fidgeted on her seat and picked absently at the muffin as I spoke.

"Well, if that's what the review said and if there was a picture to prove it, then I guess it must be true," she said flippantly.

"It's just that you had all those bags of rat poison in your garage, the same brand as in the picture."

She dropped the piece of muffin back onto the plate. "Fine. I posted the review. And I might have even paid a few other people to post bad reviews too. Everyone does it. The man set my theater on fire."

"Allegedly," I stated quietly.

"He did it. No one else believes me, but I know it was Samuels. Anyway, posting fake reviews doesn't make me a killer. And now that my alibi is solid, Detective Briggs will have to snoop somewhere else for his suspect."

She was getting red in the face. It was a good time for me to end the conversation.

"Absolutely. I'll let you finish your muffin then so you can get down to the station. Have a good day."

CHAPTER 29

*B*riggs pulled up in front of the shop and my heart did a skippity do. The relationship was still new, but I hoped that the tiny heart dance at the sight of him would never leave. My mom once told me she still got misty eyed when my dad dressed up for a special occasion. It was one of the cutest darn things the woman had ever said, and I kept every word of it in my memory.

I'd forgotten that I'd already locked up for the night. I hurried over to open the door. "What a nice surprise, James. I was just about to head home."

"Were you?" He lifted his sunglasses up to his head. "I won't keep you then."

"Nonsense." I waved him inside. "Come in off the sidewalk."

He stepped inside the shop. "I wanted to let you know the lab tests showed that Samuels had ethylene glycol in his bloodstream. That's the toxic substance in coolant. So we have our murder weapon. If I could just find out who put the coolant in the slush cup. The evidence is scant. While there seems to be numerous motives, there are also plenty of alibis."

He followed me into the office to get my purse. "I take it Connie Wilkerson visited you then?"

"Yes, how did you know?" He leaned against the door jamb while I shut down my computer.

"I just happened to run into her eating her usual Thursday morning peach muffin at Elsie's."

"Just happened, eh?" His mouth tilted on one side. "Coincidences follow you around like kids follow the ice cream truck."

I reached the doorway where he was standing. "It does seem that way, doesn't it?"

"I'll have to check out her story with the neighbor if any more evidence points to her. I'm heading back to the theater right now to talk to Dylan. He's trying to make sure everything is secure in the building until the lawyer contacts the new owners. Sally gave him her key. She didn't want the responsibility."

"Oh? I wouldn't mind going along for that. Unless you don't need your assistant tonight." I batted my lashes at him dramatically.

"I can't tell if you're trying to be coy or flirtatious or if you have something in your eye."

I smacked his arm. "Can I tag along or what?"

"Sure. That's why I stopped by."

We headed through the shop. "Where's Kingston?"

"He wanted to stay home today. We won't be too long, will we? I need to feed the pets."

"Nope. I need to feed Bear too. If he hasn't already helped himself to the coffee table."

I turned off the lights and we walked out to the car and climbed inside.

I pulled the seatbelt around me. "I was thinking maybe it's time our families meet."

Briggs' face snapped my direction. "You mean the parents?"

"No, gosh no," I said as if he'd suggested we pack up and move to the middle of the Sahara Desert. "I meant the furry family members."

Briggs checked the side view mirrors and pulled out onto Harbor Lane. "That could still include my dad. He has hair everywhere."

My laugh was cut short by a sudden thought. "Gosh, I hope *that* doesn't run in the family."

"I take after my mother's side."

"Thank goodness. Anyhow, maybe you should bring Bear over tonight. Kingston has already met him. But the big test is with Nevermore. I'm hoping Bear is still young and silly enough to not seem like a threat to Never. He doesn't mind Dash's dog, Captain," I added and quickly decided I should have kept that nugget to myself.

"I see," he said. "I'm glad because that had me worried."

"Oh stop, James. I was just using it as an example. Nevermore doesn't meet many dogs. What do you say? Should we give it a try?"

"What if they don't get along?" he asked.

It wasn't a question I expected, and I had no good answer. "It'll be fine. Nevermore is a very reasonable cat. Usually."

"If you say so, I guess I could bring Bear around later tonight."

"Perfect." I relaxed back against the seat. "What triggered this meeting with Dylan?"

"I called him to tell him about the autopsy report. He gave me an earful about going to see his mom in the hospital. He said I had no right to talk to her without asking his permission. I told him I had her doctor's permission. That seemed to satisfy him, but I think he's feeling edgy about the whole thing. I'm sure he realized his mom wouldn't corroborate his reason for the argument with his dad. He insisted it was because his mom desperately wanted to see Ronald Samuels before she went into heart surgery, but that seems far from the truth. I need to find out the real reason for the argument and find out why he lied."

"Sounds like he's back on your persons of interest list."

"He never left it." He glanced back and changed lanes. "By the way, the slush cup Samuels drank from contained the coolant. Unfortunately, condensation on the paper cup prevented any good fingerprints. The coolant container we found inside the bin had some smeared prints near the top and on the handle. One set of the same prints on both. I'm certain they'll be Justin's prints since he admitted it was his bottle of coolant. Not stellar evidence so far. I'm hoping a few more interviews will get someone to crack."

"Or maybe there is still a key piece of evidence just waiting to be uncovered," I said brightly. "You never know what might turn up."

"I like your optimism, Miss Pinkerton. I just wish some of it would rub off on me."

CHAPTER 30

The rose colored dusk sky hung low over the town of Mayfield as Briggs turned the car down Turner Boulevard. A long line of moviegoers stood outside Starlight Theater. It was easy to predict an explosion of business at Connie's theater with the Mayfield Four being indefinitely closed.

"Samuels' death sure gave Connie Wilkerson a nice boost in ticket sales," I said as we passed.

"Yes. I'd say she benefited from his death almost as if she'd been one of his benefactors. In a convoluted, disconnected way of course." The vast, empty Mayfield Four parking lot had attracted a group of kids on skateboards. They had taken the time and effort to carry a makeshift ramp to the empty lot to use for tricks.

Briggs sighed. "They know they're not supposed to be skateboarding here."

"Oh, let them stay. It's a big slab of empty asphalt. They're being resourceful. Besides, it can't be for too long. I'm sure whoever inherited the theater will open it back up soon. After all, I bet you would have done the same thing at their age."

Briggs peered sideways at me. "I preferred BMX bikes to skateboards. And since you're making me feel like an old fist shaking curmudgeon for even bringing it up, I'll ignore them."

He pulled the car up to the theater. Dylan Samuels spotted us through the tinted glass of the ticket booth. He waved and circled around to let us into the theater. "Come on in. I was just locking up all the cash drawers." He hooked the set of keys on his belt loop. "They're empty, of course, but I wanted to make sure everything was secured before I lock it up for good. My dad put his heart and soul into this place. I'd hate to see it get ruined by vandals. There's no telling when the new owners will reopen it."

"Did you find out who the new owners are?" Briggs asked. In a murder case, it was always good to find out who benefited financially from the death. It seemed we already knew of one person who would benefit. Connie Wilkerson had been struggling to compete with the Mayfield Four, but with its owner's demise, her business was going to be booming. But someone else would soon inherit Ronald Samuels' theater. Knowing who would give Briggs an entirely new path of inquiry.

"I'm in the dark about all of it." Dylan's tone darkened. "That was the way my dad did things. He kept everything to himself. My mom and I were always the last to know about anything." He straightened, stretching his barrel chest and shoulders to full width. He was a large man, but it seemed that size had never helped him feel big enough to stand up to his dad. "I suppose most men of that generation are like him. Keeping business matters to themselves and never opening up about anything."

Briggs nodded. "I suppose you're right. I do have a question for you, Mr. Samuels. When I spoke to your mother, she mentioned that she didn't want to see you dad before her operation. Or any other time, for that matter. She made that fairly clear in our brief conversation."

Dylan's jaw twitched, and he blinked more than usual. "They

didn't get along. I suppose she thought it would only aggravate her to see him."

Briggs casually pulled out his notebook. I always admired how calm and cool he stayed when he was about to start a small spark. "Of course." He flipped through a few pages. "But when I asked you about the argument overheard by some of the theater employees, you said it was because your mother would feel better if Mr. Samuels visited her before surgery. You were upset that he couldn't be bothered to see her."

Dylan's tank-sized torso shrank down, and he covered his face. "I wish you wouldn't bring up those horrible last moments." He rubbed his eyes and lowered his hand. "Do you understand how hard it is to know that our last conversation was an argument?" He was obviously trying to avoid answering. He pulled a tissue from his pocket and blew his nose.

"I'm sure it's very difficult," Briggs said and then stood waiting in resolute questioning silence. He didn't have to say a word to assure Dylan that he was still expecting a response.

Dylan got the message. He pushed the tissue, which I suspected was fairly unnecessary in the first place, back into his pocket. "I suppose it doesn't matter either way. I asked to borrow some money. I'm between jobs, and with Mom in the hospital, bills have been piling up. I thought he could help out." His face sagged with disappointment. "I was wrong. Now I have to live with those final moments knowing we never patched things up." His voice trailed off and he shook his head.

"I am sorry, Mr. Samuels," Briggs said. A light knock pulled our attention toward the glass entry doors. Justin was standing outside.

Dylan grunted. "That kid," he muttered. "He's here to pick up his last paycheck. My dad was planning to let him go this week anyhow. He was sure Justin was stealing from him. Said he found a wad of twenty dollar bills in Justin's locker. When he confronted

Justin about it, he told him he'd sold a skateboard to a friend but according to my dad, he was acting pretty cagey about it. Dad never trusted anyone, but he was probably right on this account. I never liked that kid."

Briggs and I exchanged glances as he walked to the door to let Justin in. "Guess I should talk to Justin again," Briggs said quietly from the side of his mouth. "I wonder why Samuels is only just mentioning the stealing issue."

I followed Briggs as he headed to Ronald Samuels' office. The room had remained untouched since the night of the murder. Aside from the key piece of evidence, the poisoned drink, the room had given few clues.

Briggs went to the file cabinet and pulled it open. I circled around to Mr. Samuels' desk and pulled open the first drawer. It was neatly organized with blue pens in one tray and black in another. Paper clips were layered in a neat pile next to a roll of tape. A flash of yellow caught my eye as I moved to close the drawer. A sticky note was pressed on the inside front of the drawer.

Briggs noticed me pulling it out. "Please tell me you found a note that names the murderer," he said wryly.

"Afraid not." I held it up. "It's a note Samuels wrote to himself. Fire Justin. That's all it says."

Briggs walked over and looked at it. "Seems like that is something you could remember without a sticky note. I think I'll talk to Justin before he leaves."

We left the office and found Justin looking angry and red faced as he stood toe to toe with Dylan Samuels. Dylan was holding what looked like the paycheck behind his back.

Justin spotted us walking across the lobby. He pointed at Dylan. "Detective Briggs, he won't give me my paycheck. I earned every dollar of that check. He has no right to keep it."

Dylan had apparently decided to take theater matters into his own hands. He put on a collected tone, trying to show he was the adult and that he had the upper hand of the situation. "I've simply told Mr. Lakeford that he needs to first return all the money he stole from the theater."

Justin's suntanned face turned an orange-red. "And I've told you, I never stole one dime from this place. Now give me my paycheck." Dylan was much bigger in stature than Justin, but the boy looked way more agile. His arms were sinewy but curved with muscles from surfing. I had no doubt he could throw a mean punch if he wanted. And from the look on his face, he very much wanted to do just that. Briggs' presence was probably the only thing keeping both men from throwing the first fist.

Briggs seemed to come to the same conclusion. Without an ounce of hesitation, he placed himself squarely between the two men. "Mr. Samuels, do you have any direct evidence that Justin stole from the theater?"

"No, he doesn't," Justin started angrily, but Briggs put up a hand to stop his rant.

Dylan fidgeted on his wide shoes for a moment, then shook his head. "I only know what my father told me."

"Then I need you to give me Justin's check." Briggs put out his hand. Dylan was about to smack it down on his palm but then thought better of it.

Briggs turned around and handed the check to Justin.

Justin muttered thanks and hurried toward the door.

"Hold on, Justin," Briggs called. "I need to talk to you."

Justin's shoulders sank. He spun around with one of those classic 'what now' expressions you perfect as a teen to flash at pesky parents. Slightly rude considering Briggs just snagged him his paycheck.

Briggs turned back to Dylan. "I'll let you know if there are any further developments on the case."

"Yes, that would be nice," he said bitterly. The sting of the last few minutes had turned him sour. "It seems that you aren't getting anywhere on the case."

Briggs gave him a grin that bordered on smug. "I'll find the killer. Sometimes they are hiding in plain sight." His final comment made Dylan's face darken. His eyes looked more bulgy than usual too.

I sidled up next to Briggs and walked with him toward Justin and the exit. Once outside, Briggs managed to corner Justin long enough to ask him a few questions. Justin seemed put out by the whole thing. I feared he'd be less cooperative to have two of us facing him. I stood off to the side, pretending to be interested in the movie posters hanging in the glass cases along the wall, but I kept an ear tuned to the conversation.

"Two things, Justin. I need you to find time to get to the Mayfield Police Station and leave a set of fingerprints." I peeked from the corner of my eye and saw Justin was predictably stunned by the request.

"I didn't steal any money, and I didn't poison that old grump." His voice teetered on the edge of crying.

"No, I'm not accusing you of either. I just need to confirm that the prints on the coolant bottle belonged to you."

"Of course they do. I told you, I bought it for my car. How would I be able to put coolant in my radiator without touching the bottle?"

"I know. We're looking for evidence that someone else touched the coolant. That would help us find the killer. But while I have you here, Dylan Samuels mentioned that his dad was going to fire you. He found a wad of money in your locker and thought you'd stolen it from the theater."

"Yeah, how do you like that? Samuels was nosing through everyone's lockers when the break room was empty. Must be some kind of law against that."

"Technically, they were Mr. Samuels' lockers. He was just

171

letting his employees use them. Surely, you knew he had a key to the lockers, giving him free access at any time? Sort of like the high school principals."

"Yeah, that's pretty sketchy too. Anyhow, someone else gave me that money. I didn't take it from the theater, and Samuels knew it. There was never any discrepancies between receipts and the money in the registers. He was just looking for an excuse to fire me."

"Someone else handed you a wad of twenty dollar bills?" Briggs asked.

"Yeah." Justin shrugged. "I did someone a favor and they paid me. That's all."

"Any chance I can get you to tell me the details of that favor without me having to call you in for questioning?" I was certain Briggs didn't have enough to go on to call the kid in for questioning, but the mere suggestion of it certainly sparked fear.

"Fine. I wrote a review. A bad review about the Mayfield. I mean what do I care if the place gets a bad review? Samuels deserved it. He ruined my chances to work in the surf shop. I was happy to write it."

Briggs peered briefly back toward me. "Did Connie Wilkerson pay you to write the bad review?"

"Yeah. I told her I'd do it for a hundred bucks." A half hearted laugh fell from his mouth. "Didn't think she'd take me up on it but hey, whatever. Can I go now? I'm trying to find a new job."

"Yes, and don't forget about the fingerprints. They're expecting you."

"Great. That guy is still a melted wad of gum on my shoe and he's dead." Justin turned and strutted back to his car.

Briggs joined me at the Casablanca poster. "This is where it all began." I tapped the glass over Bogie's face.

"And we never even got to finish our popcorn." He took my

hand. It was rare for him to hold it when he was on official business, but I wasn't going to complain. Far from it.

The oven-like atmosphere of the last few days was gone and a fresh cool breeze tickled the early evening air. Briggs was churning the last two conversations around in his detective's brain.

I swung my arm, taking his with it for a brief hand-clasp pendulum. "What have you concluded after talking to Justin and Dylan? Anything significant?"

He mulled over my question. "Not anything significant but I am leaning toward one person. And I'm not even sure why except my gut just keeps telling me to look that direction."

"Let me guess," I said. "Dylan Samuels?"

He looked over at me. "How did you know?"

I smiled. "I just know you too well, I guess. Plus, you left him with a rather cryptic, accusatory comment. The one about the killer hiding in plain sight. At least, if I'd been on the receiving end of it, I might have worried I was under suspicion."

Briggs opened the passenger door for me. "Good. That's exactly the effect I was going for. That way it won't be such a big shock to him when I walk up to his door with handcuffs."

CHAPTER 31

I made sure to feed Nevermore an extra helping of cat kibble. I figured if his belly was full, he'd be drowsy and happy. Nevermore wasn't prone to freak outs, but Bear was more rambunctious than most dogs. I was in the midst of my own freak out, certain that I'd pushed this meeting of the pets too quickly, when the phone rang. I sighed in relief as I rushed to it. I was sure it was Briggs letting me know he'd changed his mind. It was Lola.

"Hey, or should I say bonjour? How is it going? Must be really late there. Or early, I guess. I'll stop talking now so you can get a word in." I sealed my lips shut.

"Well, I haven't sent my parents adrift on a rudderless sailboat yet and they are still talking to me so I guess things are fine. It is beautiful here. I miss Franki's chili. Everything here is so light and frilly."

"I'll try not to be hurt by the confession that the thing you miss is a bowl of chili and not your best friend. Have you talked to your cousin? She is—she is—hmm." I paused.

"Yeah, she is," Lola said. We didn't need to fill in the blank to

174

know we were both thinking of the same nonexistent adjective. "Is she fully into her plot to try and steal Ryder away from me?"

Her question kicked my next sentence from my head where I was planning to mention that Shauna seemed to be finding numerous excuses to see Ryder. "So you expected it?"

"Yep. Growing up, Shauna was only ever interested in boys I dated. She managed to make quite the fool out of herself many times. She's five years younger. My mom and Aunt Ruby were inseparable back then, so Shauna was always at our house. One time I was sitting out on the front porch with my first boyfriend, Tate, an older man of seventeen, and Shauna came sashaying out of the house wearing one of my skirts. She had also helped herself to my makeup. I think she used all of it at once. Let's just say the circus would have hired her on the spot as a clown."

I laughed. "Her plan is more elaborate this time, and it includes poltergeists and unexplained noises, all of which require Ryder to come to the rescue."

"Actually, she is kind of a scaredy-cat, so that's not so elaborate. Anyhow, I called to see what was up with you. How is the handsome detective?"

Headlights lit up the front window. "The handsome detective," I gasped.

"Uh oh, sounds like trouble in paradise," Lola said.

"No, no trouble. It's just that I talked James into bringing Bear over to meet Nevermore. But now I'm rethinking it. Only they just pulled up so it's too late."

"Wow, you're at the pet meeting stage already? Sounds like things are heating up fast," she quipped.

"France and time with the parents hasn't dulled your sarcastic wit."

"Are you kidding? They bottle and sell sarcastic wit over here. I'll let you go. Send me pictures of Nevermore gripping the ceiling like a spider. I'll be back soon."

"All right and thanks of the confidence boost. Now I'm really regretting this. Bye. Safe flight back."

Nevermore had settled into his usual spot up on the top of the couch. His eyes were closed, and he was far off in cat dreamland. It only took Bear's first paw step on the porch to make him bolt upright.

Briggs knocked lightly, but the other sounds coming from the front porch were just a little too frightening. Nevermore shot off the back of the couch and raced down the hallway to the bedroom. I was relieved. The first cat and dog introduction could still be delayed until Bear grew more mature.

I opened the door. Bear loped right inside, ignoring Briggs' command to stay. His big, wet nose went straight to the floor, and before either of us could stop him, he galloped down the hallway, following the intriguing new scent. A carnival act followed that, under different circumstances, might have been hilarious, or at the very least worth a hundred thousand likes on Instagram. Briggs and I clashed shoulders as we both tried to squeeze through my narrow hall doorway together. We jammed together for a second, but my mother instincts kicked into super strength mode. I pushed free and shot like a torpedo down the hall to my room. I reached the doorway just as Nevermore flew out of the room (flew was not an exaggeration either. All four paws were off the ground). His fur stood up on end, and his eyes bulged as he headed for the nearest exit, the front door, which we'd left open during the chaos. The last thing I saw was his tail, looking spiky and round like a bottle brush as he vanished down the front steps.

Before either of us knew what was happening, Bear galumphed past us out the front door. We nearly repeated our cartoonish, stuck in the doorway trick but Briggs, now realizing that my cat mom adrenaline was at full throttle, waved me through first. Nevermore tore across the front lawn. His heavy dinner didn't slow him down as he quickly climbed into the branches of the spruce tree across the street. Bear reached the tree seconds before us. He was standing on his back paws, with front paws braced against the rough gray trunk, smiling happily up at the cat.

"Bear," Briggs said sternly. The dog turned his face our direction but kept his stance against the tree. Briggs pointed to the ground next to him. "Bear, heel," he said sharply. Bear's ears drooped. The big, wet smile faded as he walked, head low and paws heavy, back to Briggs.

"*Now* he listens. I'm sorry, Lacey. I was afraid this might be a bad idea. I'll put him inside the car and see if I can get Nevermore out of the tree."

"No, James, that's all right. I'll come out here with a piece of fried chicken after Never calms down. It might take thirty or forty minutes for the trauma to wear off." I turned to him. I knew my expression would give away my worry, but I just couldn't put on a fake one.

Briggs commanded Bear to stay. He obeyed. The dog seemed to understand that the fun chase through the house after the small fluffy beast had not won him a treat or an atta-boy.

"I know what you're thinking, Lacey. I can see a microscopic twitch in your nose, which means you're working hard to hold back tears."

"No, you're imaging the twitch." I looked down because I was a terrible liar, and he knew it.

He took my hand. "It'll just take time. And Bear needs to mature before he can handle something as exciting as a cat. Maybe we should start with a stuffed animal cat and work him up to the real thing. He's still in that big goober stage. Once he grows up, he'll know how to handle himself like gentleman." He looked back at Bear. The dog was sitting as still as a stone statue, except his eyes kept darting sideways toward the tree. "And he's learning to listen more. That should help."

I took a deep breath and silently chided myself for immediately thinking all was lost. "You're right, James. Next time we need to strategize better. I'm sure, eventually, they'll be the best of friends." I knew there wasn't an ounce of optimism in my tone, but I couldn't tamp down the disappointment. What if I'd finally found the man of my dreams but I had to give him up because our pets didn't get along?

Briggs held my hand tightly as we crossed the street back to my house. "I suppose I should just head home for the night, otherwise Nevermore will never come down," he suggested.

"That would probably be for the best."

He opened the back door on his car. Bear took one last gander at the tree before climbing inside. Briggs turned to me and gave me a quick kiss. He held my shoulders and looked pointedly into my eyes. "Don't over think this, Miss Pinkerton."

"I won't. I promise," I insisted with a voice that sounded anything but insistent.

He kissed my forehead. "That was the weakest sounding promise I've ever heard. I'll see you tomorrow." He opened the car door. "Call me if you need help getting the cat down from the tree."

"Oh, I don't know. I'm always looking for a reason to call one of those broad shouldered Mayfield firemen."

He squinted one eye at me. "Funny woman but I'm glad to see you smiling." He climbed into his car, started it and rolled down the window. "And everyone knows those firemen are just a bunch of hot heads."

I blew him a kiss as he rolled out of the driveway. I decided to push the evening's disaster out of my mind for now. That was going to be easier once I coaxed my neurotic cat out of the tree with fried chicken.

CHAPTER 32

*A*pparently, we were back to peonies and buttercups. I was now going to have to scramble and make a dozen calls to find a grower who could provide me with yellow and pink buttercups, or ranunculus, as they were more formally known. I wanted Jazmin to be absolutely certain before I started the search. I pulled out the example I'd created a few days ago. With all that had happened, it felt like months had passed.

After standing beneath the spruce tree holding up a cold drumstick and talking sweetly to my cat for a good half hour, he finally climbed out of the branches and followed me back inside, tail and nose in the air as if nothing had happened. He nibbled on the chicken, performed several of his masterful yoga stretches, licked his paws and toddled off to bed for the night. Briggs called to make sure the cat survived his ordeal. We ended up talking until midnight. (Which nicely counteracted the earlier disaster.)

Ryder walked in a half hour late. "Sorry, boss. I got stopped on my way here by a certain antique store clerk."

"What was it now? Furniture moving on its own?"

He laughed. "How did you know? Apparently the old Victorian pram Lola has in storage, the one she uses in her annual Christmas window display, was moving back and forth on its own. It was perfectly still and lifeless as a baby carriage should be when I walked into the storage room. I suggested that Late Bloomer might have knocked into it, setting it in motion."

"Was she satisfied with that explanation?" As we spoke, Jazmin walked in with Trinity trailing behind her.

Ryder pulled his cap off his head and fluffed up his hair with his fingers. "I honestly have no idea if she was or not, but I'm getting tired of being the local ghost buster. It would be a whole different thing if there were some actual ghosts. I mean that would be cool. But prams moving on their own and dogs moaning for lost treats? Not exactly the stuff made for television." He nodded politely to Jazmin and Trinity before heading back to the office to put his stuff away.

I waved my hand toward the bouquet. "Of course, it will look far fresher on your wedding day."

Jazmin bit her lip. Something told me a mind change would soon follow it. She walked to the bouquet and turned it around several times to look at it from every angle. She climbed up on the stool and pulled out her phone.

"Oh boy, here we go again," Trinity muttered.

"Shush," Jazmin told her. "You came here to tell Lacey something, go ahead while I take a few more pictures."

I looked expectantly at her. "What is it, Trinity?"

Trinity reached up and fiddled with a hoop earring as she looked toward Kingston's perch. "Where is your crow?"

"He likes to fly around the neighborhood in the morning and pretend he's a bird. "

She laughed. "How cute is that?" She was still staring at the empty perch, making it more than obvious that she was having second thoughts about whatever it was she wanted to tell me.

"Is there something else?" I asked.

She released a half-sigh, half-groan. "I hate being a snitch and the whole thing is silly and I'm sure it has nothing to do with the case. It's just that I noticed something kind of weird and now they are asking Justin for his fingerprints." Her rambling was stopped by a hiccough that seemed to be the result of a suppressed sob. Two more shoulder wracking hiccoughs followed.

Her older sister heard the noise. She lectured her without taking her focus off her task. "Take a few deep breaths and out with it Trinity before you work yourself into one of those annoying hiccough fits."

Trinity didn't put up her usual snarky defense and instead followed her sister's suggestion. I waited while she took a deep breath, held it and released it like a steam kettle. She went through the process two more times, then did what I liked to term the impending hiccough pause where you wait to see if they've gone away. Trinity appeared to be in the clear.

"I've got a bottle of water in the office refrigerator," I suggested.

Trinity's bangs swayed back and forth as she shook her head. "No, I'm good. I sometimes get hiccoughs when I'm nervous."

"You have nothing to be nervous about. If you don't want to tell me directly, maybe you can write it down." I wasn't about to let this go. It seemed to have something to do with the murder case. At this point, any piece of information would help move it along.

Trinity mulled over the idea of writing it but shrugged it off. "No, I'll just tell you. I'm sure it's nothing important anyhow. It's just something I'd forgotten. That was such a scary, weird night, the night Mr. Samuels died," she added in case I was thinking of a different scary, weird night. "I pushed it out of my head. But then I was thinking it was kind of strange."

Jazmin growled in frustration." Oh my gosh, Trini, just say it. Lacey has more important things to do than listen to you babble on and on with no point or purpose."

181

Trinity took a second to stick her tongue out at her sister before returning to our conversation. "I'm sure you remember that the projector was having problems that night."

"Like it was three days ago," I quipped. Jazmin giggled at my sarcasm, but it went over Trinity's head.

"When Mr. Samuels got called up to the projector room to help, he told his son he didn't have time to talk anymore. That was after I heard them yelling at each other through the concession wall. Dylan was doing what he usually did when he came to the theater, raiding the concession stand for snacks."

"Yes, I remember him coating his popcorn with parmesan cheese when I came out for the cup of water."

"That's right. You were standing there too. Mr. Samuels went up to work on the projector, and Dylan Samuels took his popcorn and walked out the door. His face was pretty red. I almost thought he was choking on a popcorn kernel or something. Right after, the counter got super busy because the movie was delayed and people came out for their free refills. But then the weirdest thing happened. We ran out of popcorn buckets, so I headed to the storage room at the end of the hallway. It's just past the employee's lounge and Mr. Samuels' office. I was staring down at the ground and nearly plowed right into Dylan Samuels coming out of the storage room. His face wasn't red anymore. It was sort of white, like a piece of paper. He didn't say anything as he scooted past me and out into the lobby. I didn't see him after that so I just assumed he left. It was weird because I'd already seen him walk out the exit but then, boom, he was there again. And of all places, inside the storage room."

"Could you tell what he was doing in there? Was anything out of place?"

Trinity shrugged. "Looked like the usual storage room packed with boxes and supplies. Not really sure why he would be in there.

I thought it was weird at the time but then Mr. Samuels was dead and the whole thing kind of flew out of my head."

Jazmin mumbled something under her breath as she browsed through the bouquet photos on her phone. I wasn't thrilled about having to chase down out of season buttercups but I was glad Jazmin had changed her mind yet again. Otherwise, Trinity might not have told me about Dylan Samuels' unexplained reappearance the night of the murder. Briggs seemed to be leaning toward Dylan as the main person of interest. Up until now he had only scant evidence and little direct motive. But I was sure the nugget Trinity just reluctantly dropped was going to be worth its weight in gold.

"Thanks for letting me know, Trinity. I'll be sure to pass on the information to Detective Briggs."

"And tell him Justin didn't kill anyone. I just know he didn't do it." Her bottom lip quivered some.

"Don't worry about Justin."

Jazmin hopped off of the stool. "I've made my decision and its final. I want to go back to the bouquet with just peonies."

Trinity looked over at me and rolled her eyes. I nearly did the same but refrained. I was a professional, after all.

CHAPTER 33

$\mathcal{J}$azmin and Trinity hadn't taken more than one step out of the shop, and I was on my phone calling Briggs. I nearly chewed off a fingernail waiting for him to answer.

"Hello, Miss Pinkerton," he said in that smooth, cool tone that made my cheeks warm.

"What took you so long to answer? I've got news, big news, giant news. In fact, expensive dinner out as a reward news."

His smooth, cool laugh had the same effect on my cheeks. "What is it? A signed confession, I hope, because I'm beating my head against a wall here."

"Nothing quite as succinct as a signed confession, but Trinity came into the shop with her sister this morning."

"Another bouquet change?"

"Yes, well sort of. She went back to the original, but that's beside the point. Trinity told me something she'd forgotten in the chaos of the night. The store is quiet, and Ryder doesn't mind watching the shop. Can we drive to the theater and I'll fill you in?"

"We could do that. Dylan mentioned that he had to turn the key into the lawyer today. I'll call him and see if he still has it."

"That's right. Dylan has the key at the moment," I said, thinking aloud. "That's all right. He has no idea why we're going back to the theater."

I heard a pair of keys clink. "I take it that the information Trinity forgot has something to do with Dylan Samuels."

"It sure does and it's a doozy. So hurry up. Not that dallying will take the dooziness factor out of it, but I'm anxious to tell you what I learned."

"I'm on my way," he said.

"Ryder, I'm going to take off with James for a bit. Can you hold down the fort?"

Ryder looked up from the rose arrangement he was making and glanced around the empty shop. "I think I can handle it."

I chuckled. "Just enjoy this slow period. The holidays are around the corner." I stepped outside. My bird swept down from the roof and landed at my feet. "I thought you'd run off to marry a carrier pigeon or something." I opened the door. "Look who has decided to grace us with his presence. Make sure he gets some snacks. I'm sure he's extra hungry after his adventure."

"King, ole buddy," Ryder said as I closed the door.

Briggs pulled up to the curb. He was on the phone as I climbed inside. "Yes, that would be great. If it's not too much trouble. We're heading there right now. Thanks." He hung up. "Dylan had already turned in the key. I talked to Ronald Samuels' lawyer. He gave the key to the new owner. They are meeting us at the theater to open up. I'm sure whoever inherited the theater is anxious to get this murder case solved, so the rumors and bad press can stop."

"Did the lawyer say who the new owner was?" I asked.

"Nope. I told him I needed to get inside. I didn't tell him why." Briggs looked over at me. "Because I don't actually know why."

I turned slightly in my seat to face him. "Trinity was agitated and worried to tell me because she knew she had left out some-thing pretty important. Although, I doubt she realized it at first. But she's so worried about Justin being a suspect, it seemed to jog her memory of that night."

He stared out the front window, but it wasn't the mostly empty road he was focused on. His unshaven jaw moved side to side in thought.

"Why do I have the distinct feeling I'm about to get my bubble burst and lose out on an nice dinner to boot?"

"No, sorry. It's just that if her motive for suddenly remem-bering something crucial came out of her fear that her boyfriend would be arrested for murder, we might have to take it with a grain of salt."

I twisted back to face front and slumped against the seat. "Well poop. I guess you just showed me why I'm not sitting in the driver's seat wearing my detective's suit and tie. That didn't even occur to me."

"Or I could be entirely wrong and she just forgot. After all, I'm sure it was the first time she had been witness to a murder. What did she have to say?"

"All right, I'll tell you, but the wind has been taken right out of my sails."

He reached over and squeezed my hand. "What if I still promise to take you to a nice dinner?"

I sat up straight. "Yep, the wind is back. Trinity told me that she watched Dylan walk out of the theater, red in his face and angry, after his dad told him their conversation was done. Then Ronald Samuels went up to the projector room and Dylan left. After a busy rush on soda refills at the counter, Trinity left the concession stand to get more popcorn buckets from the storage room." I paused. "Did the team search that room?"

"The storage room? Yes. It's at the end of the hallway past

Samuels' office. It was mostly stacks of unopened supply boxes. They didn't find anything of note. Why do you bring it up?"

"Trinity claims that as she headed into the storage room, Dylan was walking out. She added that he looked white as paper too."

"But she saw him leave the theater?"

"Yes. That's why she thought it was weird. He left but something made him come back."

Briggs nodded. "If her story is accurate, then that is a pretty explosive detail. Can't believe she left that out when we interviewed her."

"Maybe she just didn't think it was important," I said.

"At least not until Justin was asked to give fingerprints. Which he did, by the way. His prints were on the coolant. Only his." We drove along Turner Boulevard. The Starlight was offering two popcorns for the price of one and a free bag of gummy worms with every ticket.

"Looks like Connie's business is doing well enough to toss in some freebies," I noted. "Wait until she hears that the new owner has been given the keys."

Briggs pulled into the empty Mayfield Four parking lot. The skateboard ramp and the skaters were gone. I glanced over at Briggs.

"Don't look at me. I'm sure the local police told them to move their skate park elsewhere. But it wasn't this grumpy old fun destroyer."

I sat back with a satisfied smile. There was one more car in the parking lot, a bright blue Toyota.

"I know that car," Briggs said. "I wonder—It can't be. Maybe it's true."

"Care to cut me in on your odd conversation?" I asked.

Briggs parked the car and pointed through the windshield. "Looks like the new owner is here already. Look who it is."

I squinted through the sunlight reflecting off the glass to the

187

shadowy entrance of the theater. Sally Applegate was unlocking the theater door.

"Sally? Do you think Samuels left everything to his assistant manager?"

"Seems that way." Briggs turned off the car and unfastened his seatbelt.

"Does that give her a motive?" I asked. "Or maybe they were seeing each other," I suggested.

"Neither. When I talked to the lawyer, he said he'd only just informed the new owner. He mentioned the person was extremely shocked and thrilled. I don't think Sally knew."

I unfastened my seatbelt. "Well, well. Maybe Mr. Samuels wasn't such a terrible guy after all. Sally is taking care of a sick mom and struggling to make ends meet." We climbed out of the car. "So Dylan is still at the top of the list?" I asked.

"He never left it," Briggs said. "Now let's see if we can find something to prove he did it."

CHAPTER 34

Sally Applegate let us into the theater and then drifted around in her flowy batik dress gazing at the lobby like a kid lost in a candy shop. "I can't believe this is happening. It's too much to absorb." Her words might have been meant for us, but it was hard to tell because they floated up and away as she twirled slowly around.

"Congratulations, Sally," I said. "I think you'll make this place better than ever."

She stopped her semi-dance and smiled at both of us. "I still can't believe he left this to me."

Briggs cleared his throat lightly. A signal that he was getting down to business, which for him meant solving the murder. "The lawyer mentioned that you had no idea Mr. Samuels left the theater to you."

"I never would have guessed in a million years. Frankly, he was just never that nice to me. I was convinced he didn't even like me but kept me on because no one else wanted to work for him. But the lawyer told me Mr. Samuels said it should go to me because I would take good care of the theater." Her voice broke. She pressed her fingertips to her lips. "Excuse me. It's just that this is so overwhelming."

"I'm sure it will take some time to get used to," Briggs said. "I'm certain it will be much better for business if we find the person who poisoned Mr. Samuels. If we could just take a look around one more time."

"Of course. I'm sorry. I forgot why you came. Please feel free. Like you said, the quicker you arrest the murderer, the better."

"Thank you." Briggs and I headed toward the hallway with the office and storage room. There was a brown metal door at the end of the hallway that said emergency exit. Briggs opened it and peered outside into the alley. "That's what I thought. This leads right to the trash bin."

He opened the storage room door and switched on the light. It was just as I expected, a small closet like room with metal shelves packed high with unopened cartons of popcorn kernels, candy treats and paper goods. The one wide open box was filled with latex gloves.

"You take the right side and I'll take the left, and we'll meet in the middle," Briggs said with a wink.

"Right. The right. What are we looking for exactly?" I asked.

"Not too sure. Something that looks out of place. Something that would explain Dylan's unexpected visit to the storage room."

Most of the boxes were taped shut, waiting to be opened, which in a way was a blessing. It would have taken all day to search through every box. "I assume that if the box is still sealed shut, we don't need to look inside."

"Right. Unless it looks like it's been unsealed and sealed back up." He reached into a shelf. "Like this box of straws." He tore free the masking tape someone had pulled over the box to seal it after the packing tape had been broken. "Just straws." He taped the box shut.

I found one opened carton that contained Milk Duds. "Yum, my childhood favorite." I plucked out a box and shook it. Nice and hard too. Making it the perfect candy for removing unwanted fillings or loose teeth." I stuck the box back into the carton but couldn't get it to go all the way down so that it was flush with the rest of the boxes. I pulled it out to turn it the other way. That was when a whiff of something other than Milk Duds tickled my nose. I pulled the box closer to the edge and put my face near to catch the scent again.

"Briggs, I've got something. Unless Milk Duds have changed their formula—" I pulled the entire box free of the shelf and set it on the ground. Briggs joined me as I crouched down to get a look inside the box under the light.

My face popped up. "Latex gloves?"

He reached into his pocket and pulled out a pair of tweezers. "Sure looks that way." He plucked out the latex gloves that were jammed into the space between the candy boxes. As he drew them free, a faint scent drifted toward me.

"Coolant," I said. "Even though they are turned inside out, I can smell coolant. And something else, but I'm not sure what."

Briggs couldn't hold back a smile. "What would I do without Samantha? And the cute Miss Pinkerton attached to her, of course."

"Of course. I'll make sure to order a lush dessert with my expensive dinner to reward Samantha."

Briggs held the gloves in the tweezers. "You can order any dessert you want."

Briggs searched in his pocket with his free hand and pulled out an evidence bag. I leaned to the side and looked at his pocket. "What else do you have in those endless pockets, Inspector Gadget?"

"I think that's about it. With any luck and a lot of science, we'll be able to lift some prints off the inside of the gloves." He handed me the bag to open. I held it out for him. As he dropped the gloves inside, the second odor came to me.

"Parmesan cheese. How could I not tell that was parmesan. There are few aromas like it."

Briggs looked puzzled. "Why are you talking about parmesan cheese?"

"Because I can smell it on the inside of the gloves." I snapped my fingers. "And Dylan Samuels was eating popcorn with parmesan just before his father was killed. I saw him pouring it on his popcorn. Loads of it."

Right then, agitated voices rolled down the hallway to the storage room.

"I can't believe this," a man yelled. "How could he do this?" I'd never heard him yell before, but it was easy to recognize that the agitated man was Dylan Samuels.

"Sally," I gasped.

Briggs nearly dropped the bag in his rush to get out to the lobby. Dylan Samuels was pacing with a face as red as a tomato. His nostrils were flared like an angry bull's. Sally stood behind the concession counter, apparently trying to put space between her and the angry man in the center of the lobby.

I walked over to stand with Sally. Dylan spotted Briggs. He lifted an arm and pointed angrily at him. "And you, you incompetent fool. I might just sue your police department for incompetence. When will you find my dad's killer?"

Briggs stepped into the lobby. "Actually, I've found him."

The red rage in Dylan's face drained. "You have? Where is he?"

"Dylan Samuels, I'm arresting you for the murder of Ronald Samuels."

Dylan stood there listening to his rights being read and looking almost sad enough to make me feel sorry for him.

"He was a monster. He verbally abused my mother and me for years and then cut us out of his will. I didn't plan it. The judge will see that. It was a moment of extreme anger. I saw the coolant so I ran inside and got his drink." He dropped down to his knees. "I almost didn't put the drink back in his office. But he wouldn't even lend me money to pay bills. I'm his only son." He crumpled further, his thick shoulders folding in on him as his head dropped forward. "I was his only son," he muttered again.

The sorry sight brought tears to Sally's eyes. I put my arm around her shoulder.

CHAPTER 35

*R*yder burst into the shop so exuberantly the goat bell fell off. He was holding an extra large book with a frayed and tattered cover in one arm as he bent down to retrieve the fallen bell.

He attempted to tie it back onto its ribbon with one hand but gave up and carried it with him to the work island. "Look what Lola brought me from France. It's dated 1885. It's filled with fantastic lithographs of flowering plants."

I gently lifted the cover. The binding along the edge of the book was worn from time and use, and I feared the book would fall apart if I wasn't careful. "Wow, the pictures are stunning, Ryder. It's gorgeous."

Ryder was beaming from ear to ear. Lola had left suddenly and it had hurt him plenty, but it seemed she'd made up for her abrupt departure with one magnificent, thoughtful gift.

"I'm anxious to say hello too," I said. "Is she already across the street?"

"Yes, she just opened up. Shauna packed up last night and went home. I let Lola know that there are a lot of ghosts and ghouls hanging around her antique shop and that I was now officially a ghost hunter if she needed help."

"I think we'll have to get you a pair of coveralls with a ghost buster badge. I'm going to head over there and say hello." I walked out into the bright day. The heat wave had been over for a week. There was even the tiniest touch of fall in the air which excited me.

I walked inside. Lola was moving glassware around in the shelf to make room for a few new items.

"So are you fluent in French?" I asked.

She spun around. "Pink!" We hugged.

"So good to see you," I said. "When we have time I want to see pictures and hear stories. How are your parents?"

"They're fine. I realized as I grow older, I can tolerate hanging out with them much more."

"I'm finding the same thing," I said. "I was homesick after my parents left Port Danby last month. I guess we're both really growing up."

"I don't know about that." She pointed down to her signature style. Today's outfit included a faded Grateful Dead t-shirt, shorts and cowboy boots. "My mom tried to buy me some new clothes in Paris, but I wasn't interested. Speaking of Paris, I spent hours in an old bookstore."

"Ryder is floating around the shop with little wings on his shoes. It was the perfect gift for him."

"I've got something for you too." She disappeared into the back for a second and returned with a book shaped package wrapped in a Paris newspaper and twine.

"I do love gifts that come wrapped in French newspapers. Of course this is my first, but I already know I love them." I slipped off the twine and carefully pulled away the paper. The book was old and bound in embossed, bronze tinted leather. "Edgar Allen

Poe, *The Raven and Other Poems*. I love it. It's perfect." We hugged again.

"It's not first edition but it's quite old. Someone named Margaret gave it to her brother James for Christmas in 1920. There's a handwritten note on the inside cover."

"James?" I asked. "Even more perfect."

"Glad you like it. So what have I missed? Anything interesting happen while I was gone?"

"Oh, you know, the usual. Murder, peonies, poison, that kind of stuff. We'll go have a bowl of chili at Franki's later, and I'll tell you all about it."

CLUTTER COOKIES

View recipe online at www.londonlovett.com/recipe-box

Clutter
COOKIES

Ingredients:

1 cup light brown sugar
3/4 cup granulated sugar
1 cup (2 sticks) butter, softened
2 eggs
2 tsp vanilla
2 1/4 cup all-purpose flour
3/4 teaspoon baking soda
1/2 teaspoon kosher salt

6oz semi-sweet chocolate, roughly chopped
4oz white choclate, roughly chopped
1/3 cup dried cranberries, chopped
1/3 cup toffee bits
1/3 cup chopped pecans
1/3 cup chopped walnuts
1/2 cup oats

Directions:

1. Preheat oven to 325°

2. In a stand mixer or by hand whip softened butter, brown sugar and granulated sugar until light and fluffy.

3. Beat the 2 eggs into the mixture and add vanilla.

4. Add salt, baking soda and flour. Mix just enough to combine.

5. Fold in the chocolate, cranberries, nuts, toffee bits and oats.

6. Using a 1/4 cup measuring cup scoop the dough onto a greased or parchment lined baking sheet. (Note: 1/4 cup makes the giant sized cookies seen in the pictures. You could also make smaller cookies.)

7. Bake for 15-17 minutes until the edges begin to brown and tops are dry. (Note: If you're making smaller cookies you'll need to adjust this time.)

8. Remove from oven, transfer to a cooling rack and ENJOY!

There's more Port Danby cozies coming soon . . . in the meantime . . .

Looking to try something a little different? Check out my cozy mystery series that has a fun paranormal twist!

Now Available

ABOUT THE AUTHOR

If you enjoyed **Peonies and Poison** please consider leaving a quick review. Each and every review, no matter how long is incredibly helpful and greatly appreciated.

London Lovett is the author of both the Port Danby and Firefly Junction Cozy Mystery series. She loves getting caught up in a good mystery and baking delicious, new treats!

Join London Lovett's Secret Sleuths!

facebook.com/groups/londonlovettssecretsleuths/

Subscribe to London's newsletter at www.londonlovett.com to never miss an update.

London loves to hear from readers. Feel free to reach out to her on Facebook: Facebook.com/londonlovettwrites

Follow on Instagram: @londonlovettwrites
Or send a quick email to londonlovettwrites@gmail.com.

Follow London

www.londonlovett.com
londonlovettwrites@gmail.com